KIRA BLACK

Printed in Australia

Cover and internal design by Shawline Publishing Group Pty Ltd

First printing: March 2024

Shawline Publishing Group Pty Ltd

www.shawlinepublishing.com.au

Paperback ISBN 978-1-9229-9367-0

eBook ISBN 978-1-9229-9378-6

Distributed by Shawline Distribution and Lightning Source Global

Shawline Publishing Group acknowledges the traditional owners of the land and pays respects to the Elders, past, present and future.

A catalogue record for this work is available from the National Library of Australia

DARK Desires

KIRA BLACK

Dedications

Nephy – my rock and support, without you I
would have lost my mind.
Hayley – thank you for making sure I ate, for loving
me and supporting the writing process.
TDA – y'all know who you are, the family I
didn't know I needed or had.
I love you all. Thank you for being who you are.

Prelude

You know that feeling when you meet someone and you just click right away? When you're comfortable being quiet with them right there, with that safe feeling you get from hearing their voice, hearing them breathe, just being near them? That feeling that they're the one, they're the piece that was missing that you didn't even realise was missing until it's right there in front of you?

There's all these people in the world – billions of them – so finding that one person is rather hard. Sometimes you feel you've got the right one, but it's never quite right. It works - you love them, laugh with them, have a good connection with them – but it's just not enough. There's a… spark missing, that little bit of life, something extra that you know you should have and try hard to bring it to what you have but it is always just out of grasp.

Well, that's my life. It's full but not; it's amazing yet missing something. Until I met him. We met almost eight years ago now, spent time talking on the phone, video calling and really getting to know each other over a few years. We weren't even geographically close until I took a leap of faith, went to visit and never left.

We have been together since and every day, even the bad ones, is a good day. We clicked. I found that piece that was missing. He is everything I dreamed of but never dared to dream all at once…

Let me take you back to the beginning.

⚭ Chapter 1 ⚭

My name is Marie. I've been working the same job for the same company for more years than I care to remember. My life is rather routine: work, home, work, shopping, work and so on. One night, while off on holidays, I decide to set up a dating profile, but why only look at local people? I open it up to the world. I don't really think too much about it at the time. I look at it once in while but nothing really happens and I forget about it, going back to my routines.

About two months or so after opening it, I receive a notification – reading, 'You have a message' – from the dating app. I ignore it at first. I was busy and thought it was just telling me I had been inactive. When I get home that night, I'm scrolling my notifications on my phone, which spends most of the day on 'do not disturb', when I see the reminder. I click it. There is a message there, alright. My heart races.

Hello, my name is Mike. I saw your picture and thought you were beautiful. I hope you reply. I would like to get to know you.

I stare at my phone, completely dumbfounded for a good ten minutes, when I finally work up the nerve to click his profile. It's as if I thought he could see me – I want to face-palm my forehead! As soon as I see his eyes my heart skips a beat. So much in those eyes. I can't help myself; I spend the next thirty minutes reading his profile and looking at the few pictures he had there. I decide I have nothing to lose and send him a message back.

Hi, Mike, my name is Marie. Thank you for your lovely compliment. I would like to get to know you as well.

I click send and place my phone on the coffee table. My hand is shaking; I need a drink and a cigarette. What am I thinking? Some random person sends me a message on a dating site and I answer! Another face-palm moment, Marie, well done! I absently pick my phone up as I walk outside to have my cigarette. *Ding.* The sound makes my heart leap into my chest! I look down at my phone and there's a message from the dating app. My jaw drops slightly. I open the app to see a message from Mike.

Hola, Marie! I am so glad you messaged back. I didn't think you would. I've had this app for so long and have never messaged anyone before. But as soon as I saw your picture, I just couldn't scroll past it. To be honest, it took me three days just to work the nerve up to send the short message to say hello. I didn't in my wildest dreams think I would get a response. Oh, I'm rambling, sorry! Thank you for making my day a little brighter. Mike.

I must read that message ten times before I place my phone on my outside table as far as I can get it without throwing it on the floor. My cigarette has burnt away to nothing, and I haven't had more than one or two drags. I roll another one as I contemplate what I had re-read so many times. I feel a little thrill run through my body. This random man thinks I'm beautiful. It has been years since I've heard that, let alone read that. I pick my phone up again and read the message. Should I reply? Should I just leave it? I am intrigued to say the least. I start writing a message back.

Hiya, Mike. I had a look at your profile and noticed you have a dog. He/she is beautiful, what breed? What do you do for work? I'm an administrative officer in a hospital. Mind-numbing! But I've been there for years. I like the work and the people aren't so bad. By the way, you have amazing eyes, the type a person could get lost in for days given half a chance. I found myself staring at them for a long while... now look who's rambling. Lol. Marie x

Oh lord! Did I just send an 'x'? I sent a kiss to a guy I've sent two messages to! I must be losing it. I close my phone and throw it on the couch as I walk back inside. Three face-palm moments in one night, you're on a roll, Marie. I walk into the kitchen and pour a drink. It's still early, seven p.m. I need to clear my head and take a deep breath.

Ding. I almost drop my glass. I eye my phone like it's going to bite me. *Ding.* Two messages! I walk over to the couch and pick the phone up. I hold it away from me like he can see when I'm looking at it. I'm being ridiculous! I open the messages…

Hi, Marie, thanks for the compliments about my eyes! They go alright. My dog is my best friend – she goes everywhere with me. Her name is Susie, she's a shepherd and she's almost eight years old now. Do you have any animals? Mike.

Oh, I almost forgot, I am an instructor. I teach ppl how to scuba dive. Mike. x

He sent an 'x' back. I'm going to need a stronger drink at this rate! I take my drink, grab my cigarettes and head back outside. I read all the messages again. He seems friendly. What's the harm in getting to know someone over a dating app? I light my cigarette and think about things a little longer. Without even realising I'm doing it, I am back looking at this man. Brown hair, green eyes, five days of growth on his face, a cute smile… I could see myself with him.

I laugh at myself. Way to go, Marie, living in a fantasy before you even know where he is and if he's married. Oh my god, what if he's married?! Lord, wait till I talk to Tash! Natasha is my best friend. we don't live close, but we talk every day and call each other on weekends. She's my rock and I consider her my sister. She knows more about me than anyone in my life, including family. We can spend hours talking and laughing. Tash is the kind of person who sees only your good qualities and embraces your not-so-good ones. As she told me once, 'Marie, you aren't you without the dark places. You can't always be light and air – sometimes you need to be dark and scary too! Either way, I love you.' She just gets me.

Hi! She's a beautiful dog. Scuba diving sounds like a fun job! Although sharks scare me… A LOT. Lol. So where are you in the world? Do you have a favourite drink? Atm I'm drinking vodka, lime and soda water. It's Friday for me and it's nice to unwind with a drink and have a cigarette. Please don't judge me for smoking, I know the risks. It's my one bad vice… well, it's not but it's the worst one, I think, lol! Anyways, now I'm rambling! ~Marie xo

I stare at my phone, I did it again! And this time I added a hug. What the fuck is wrong with me?! If that doesn't scream 'desperate' I don't know what does! I need to call Tash! I check the time; it's eight p.m. here so it must be close to eleven p.m. where she is. Ahhh fuck it, I know she'll be awake, she's always awake. I pick the phone up and call Tash.

'Hello, gorgeous.' As soon as I hear her voice, I know what she's going to say when she hears what I've been up to.

'Hi, babe! Did I wake you?' She laughs at me. I knew she'd be awake.

'You know I wasn't sleeping. I was rearranging my rocks. So what's new in your world?'

I take a deep breath. 'Well, remember that dating app I downloaded and then did nothing with?'

She makes a non-committal sound.

'I got a message from a guy today. His name is Mike.' Silence for a spilt second...

'Tell me EVERYTHING!' she practically yells down the phone at me.

I spend the next three hours telling her what little I know about Mike and by the end of the call I'm feeling a lot better about the whole thing. It feels right when Tash says to see where it goes and enjoy the ride. It could be the best thing I've ever done. I guess time will tell.

I shut my phone off and leave it in the kitchen to charge overnight. Three hours on the phone and four or five drinks and I'm ready for bed. Tash got me thinking and after all her reasons to go for it, my reasons not to paled in comparison. As I climb into bed and close my eyes, I can't help but daydream a little about what it could be like with someone laying right here next to me. I fall asleep all warm and fuzzy inside, a slight smile on my face.

Chapter 2

Good lord my head hurts! I roll out of bed, stumble to the kitchen and make coffee. I walk outside and light a smoke. It's still early – maybe five a.m. – the sun is just peaking over the roof tops, there is a light breeze, the birds are singing their good mornings to the world and the air is warm. I have a few messages from Tash who has probably slept for a maximum of three hours in the last twenty-four. I don't know how she does it. I answer her and continue scrolling my notifications. I nearly drop my phone when I see there are four messages from Mike! I open the app, scrolling the messages – just general chit chat. I drink my coffee and finish my cigarette. I'm lost in a daydream when I hear that familiar *ding*. I snatch up my phone so fast.

Good morning, Marie. I am assuming it's morning there anyway. You never told me where you are. Anyway, I hope this finds you well and I hope to hear from you soon. Mike xo.

I rock back a little in my chair. Why did that just make me feel all warm and fuzzy inside? There's nothing really in it and the ones before that were just the same. Idle chit-chat and no real context, he is just telling me about his day as it happens. I find myself scrolling through the messages again. Something is drawing me in, I just haven't put my finger on it yet. He is handsome, he seems sweet in the messages, no real red flags, he isn't pushing for information and seems happy to just talk. I need a shower, I feel gross. I'll answer when I feel something closer to normal.

Thanks to everything holy for plumbing and instant hot water! I'm starting to feel more like Marie and less like something that dragged itself out of the gutter after a hard night on the town. That thought has me thinking about Tash again. I miss our nights of debauchery – we used to wreak havoc. It might be time to go visit her. *Ding.* The sound pulls me out of my daydream.

Hello again. Sorry I'm bombarding you with messages. I'm not sure what it is about you, but every time I look at your picture, I am drawn to you. You have beautiful eyes and a great smile. I hope to hear from you soon. Mike xoxo

Oh! There's that feeling again! How did he do that? I want to know everything about this guy and I've been talking to him for less than twenty-four hours.

Good morning, Mike! My eyes are beautiful? Have you been drinking? Lol. It's 6.35 a.m. here at the moment. I've just had a shower and am starting to feel human once again. I don't think I told you where I am, but let's get to know each other a little more first. Marie xoxo

I start doing all the things I need to for my day and spend a good hour talking to my mother. Lord, that woman can prattle on about nothing! I finish the dishes, put the washing on and move on to other things that I've been putting off for a good week. I find myself checking my phone more often than not, waiting for that sound. I need a distraction. I pick up a book and start reading, hoping to immerse myself in someone else's fantasy. It works for a little while until I read the sex scene and then my mind makes the crazy leap to Mike. I can't seem to stop thinking about him. I can feel myself getting wet just at the thought of that man's hands on my body!

I slide my hand down into my pants; I can feel how wet I am. I start rubbing my clit in little circles. God, that feels good. I bring up a picture of Mike and, after studying for a minute, I lean back and close my eyes, imagining that face buried in my pussy, tongue sliding into my wetness. I rub my clit a little faster, moaning. I arch my back as I get closer to toppling over the edge. My imagination runs away with me, seeing Mike's hands sliding up my body, squeezing my nipples, his finger slipping into me… OMG, yessssss! I cum. *Ding.* That sound drags me back to reality in a hurry. Did he know I was looking at his picture? I try to collect my thoughts that I just scattered all over my couch! I pick up my phone that I dropped as I was cumming.

Well, hello there. Why are you awake so early? I'm a fan of a good sleep in. I am currently on my day off. I think I'm going to have a few drinks and watch some sports. Do you have any plans for your evening? Yes, your eyes are amazing. Just so you know, the whole package is beautiful. If I don't hear from you before I go to bed, thank you for being a part of my day. Mike xoxo

Did he thank me for being a part of his day? That was really sweet!

Hi, Mike! I was just thinking about you! He doesn't need to know I was cumming while doing it… *It's about lunchtime here. I'm currently on vacation from work for the next three weeks, so I might have a drink with you. What sport are you watching? I know a little about football but not much about anything else. Hope to hear from you soon. Marie xoxo*

I stare at my phone. I seriously wanna give this guy my number so I can see when he's texting me back! Oh my god, that sounded desperate even to me! I need Tash. I pick up my phone and make a call.

'Hello, sweet cheeks!' Tash always sounds so happy.

'Hiya, Tash! I'm calling you to prevent me giving my number to this guy!' I laugh.

'What's the problem with that? Do it!'

I snort. Maybe I shouldn't have called Tash. 'Are you high? I can't be giving my number to random guys I just met on a dating app! What is wrong with you?'

She laughs at me; it sounds like a bell pealing. 'Yeah, I guess, 'cause you've got people lining up out your door trying to get a little of what you are letting grow over!'

Did she just call me a born-again virgin?! 'Tash!' I exclaim.

'Well? What have you got to lose? You don't know if he's even close by. It's not like he is going to show up on your doorstep!'

She has a point. God damn it, she's always right! 'Yeah, you're right! Fuck it, I'll give him my number next time he sends me a message.'

'That's my girl! Now go be the hoe I love! Bye, bye, sweet cheeks!' She literally hangs up on me knowing I would pummel her with questions. Ass! Tash knows me too well. That said, that woman has been there through many a sad bitch hour with me. I couldn't ask for more from her. *Ding.*

Hola! I'm watching football tonight, but I watch most sports. My favourite would be hockey. Do you watch sport? So three weeks off! Nice! Do you have plans? I guess not as most of the world is off limits at the moment. I went to Canada for my last vacay; it was amazing! You know what will make this easier? Being able to actually talk to you. Let me know if you'd like to exchange numbers. Talk soon sweetheart. xoxo

Did he hear my phone call?! He called me sweetheart! I swear I swooned. I feel my heart melt a little. That man has all the right words, so much right. I make a cup of tea and contemplate his message. He seems so sweet and genuine. He isn't pushy, hasn't asked for nudes, hasn't made me uncomfortable and, let's face it, I just got off to his picture! I need therapy or sex... I haven't decided which, probably both and, knowing me, my therapist would need their own therapy straight after! I walk back to the lounge and pick up my phone and send him my number. Nothing else, just my number. He'll either call or he won't. I take my tea and walk outside for a smoke.

My phone rings. I nearly drop it! I'm so confused. I don't recognise that number! I just sit there staring at it. I place it on the table and watch it vibrate across it. I've never been one for answering unknown numbers. If it's important they will leave a voicemail. But I have no idea who would be calling me from another country! It's probably telemarketers or that fake tax office bullshit! It stops ringing. *Ding.* Oh, a message! My heart jumps a little bit as open the message.

I sincerely hope you gave me the right number! LOL. Mike.

Oh fuck!

OMG I'M SO SORRY! I didn't recognise the number! I'm sorry. I've got it now. I'll add it to my phone to prevent it happening again! Marie.

Another face palm moment. How did I not click that it was Mike calling me? *Ding.*

Well, I guess now that you have my number you can call me back! Hope to hear from you soon! Mike xxoo

Well, fuck! I'm instantly nervous. This random guy is making me feel stuff I haven't felt in forever, or even ever! Now he has thrown a massive curve ball into my court and I have to call him! FUCKKKK! I roll a smoke with shaking hands. Why are they shaking? I try to light it but can't make the lighter work. God damn it woman, get a grip! You've spoken to random people before, what is wrong with you? I try the lighter again and get it to work. Slamming it back onto the table, I try to calm down. I bring up his profile. Just looking at those eyes still makes me nervous and something else I haven't quite figured out yet. I draw on my cigarette and study the man I'm seeing. There is nothing remotely scary about him yet I feel… scared? No, it's not scared, it's something else. I look a little harder. His eyes catch me. There is something in those damn eyes. It's like he can look right through me even though it's just a picture. It feels like he can see me, the real me without even trying. *Ding.*

Are you going to call me back? Mike.

Shit, how long had I been stuck in thought?

Hi, Mike. Sorry, yes, I'll call you back. When is good? Marie xx

I stare at my phone wide eyed, why did I say that? *Ding.*

Now! I'm looking forward to it!

My heart is racing, I check the time and walk straight to the kitchen. I pull my vodka out of my freezer and pour myself a strong drink; I'm going to need some liquid courage for this! Lord, how I wish Tash was here to kick my ass a little. This isn't even hard! I down my drink and make another. I walk out to the table and I pick my phone up. There's that picture again, those eyes, I dial the number… it rings.

Chapter 3

I almost hang up. It's only rung twice but with each ring, my nerves escape me a little more.

'Hello.' Oh my, that voice!

'Hi, Mike.'

'Marie! It's so nice to hear your voice.' He sounds so genuine.

I can't believe I am talking to this guy. I need to stop calling him 'this guy'. Mike. His voice is sweet, yet sexy, a little husky. I am completely taken aback. I can't place the accent yet, although I must sound terrible to his ears. There's no hiding an Australian accent no matter where you are in the world.

'Call me Mike.'

'I'm just Marie, but it works for the most part. I haven't been late for dinner once!'

Oh my god, that laugh! I put my phone on speaker so I can roll a smoke. I light the smoke and he must have heard the lighter.

'I might join you in a smoke.'

'Oh, you smoke? You didn't say. Although I guess I didn't ask either.'

'No, you just told me not to judge.' He laughs and I feel everything in me tighten up.

'You have an amazing laugh!' I say without thinking. Mike goes quiet for a hot minute.

'Thank you, I guess. No one has ever said that before.' The next sound he makes almost makes me gasp. It's the cutest sound, halfway between a laugh and a chuckle.

I laugh so much during our call. This man is funny and sweet, he listens and is kind of all the things I want and a little more. It was shit that the call had to end at all but it was getting late where he was, which I finally found out was Bora Bora. His accent sounded different though. I am going to have to find out exactly where this man is from. I look at the clock – eleven p.m.

'Alright, sweetheart, I need to get some sleep. It's three a.m. here.'

'Oh, holy shit, I'm so sorry! It's only eleven p.m. here, although I've drunk way more than I should have.' I laugh, feeling the alcohol.

'Don't be silly. I enjoyed my time with you tonight. Thank you for being a part of my day.' Be still my heart – did he just thank me for being a part of his day again?! Who even does that? I can't stop smiling.

'No problems. It's been so much fun!' I hope he can hear the sincerity in my voice.

'Goodnight, Marie.'

'Goodnight, Mike.'

I hang the phone up and sit there smiling like an idiot. That call must have lasted six to eight hours easily. He is so easy to talk to! I check the time. My god, it's late. I go upstairs to my room and fall into bed, a smile planted firmly on my face.

I wake up at five a.m. as always and make a coffee. I'm still rubbing sleep out of my eyes when I finally pick up my phone and see text messages from Mike on there and not just one either – four of them. I open the texts and smile instantly. The first one is a photo of him sitting on the beach with his dog Susie, with the caption, *Good morning beautiful* under it. Two more photos of the sunrise where he is and a short text saying, *I really enjoyed talking to you last night. I can't wait to hear your voice again.*

I smile at my phone. I look at the pictures for a while. It's just gorgeous where he is! My mind wanders thinking about that for a while. Why has this guy got me so hooked already? I sit at my outdoor table and let my mind wander to random thoughts – what colour does he like, what's his favourite food, favourite drink, how does he have his coffee? Why would I need to know that! I mean, the chances of meeting are slim to none. Maybe I should just enjoy the journey and forget about the final destination. Take a leaf out of Tash's book and live in the moment. I answer his text.

Good morning, Mike! What a beautiful place you live in! I am jealous. Talk soon!

I go about doing all the things that I need to get done. I decide that I need to send him a photo of me. Lord, I haven't taken a selfie in forever! I find a good angle, take multiple selfies and despise all of them. I swear I've aged a good ten years in the last two. After many, many photos, I finally decide on one that looks half decent. I send it and instantly get apprehensive.

OMG, you are gorgeous!

The instant reply makes my heart soar.

Thank you!

This begins hours and hours of conversation via text messages. I laugh so hard – he is funny, smart, caring, sweet and let's face it, who doesn't love a guy that can make you laugh! I ask all the questions I want answers to and answer all of his. To be honest, it is like we are getting reacquainted, more than learning new things about a person we haven't met before. The texts go on for hours. In the end Mike calls me.

'Hello!'

'Good evening. I find this easier. Texting is hard with fat fingers.' He laughs.

That laugh makes things tingle that shouldn't be tingling when someone laughs. Without a conscious thought, a slight, quiet moan escapes my lips.

'Well, that's the prettiest sound I've heard all day.' His voice is husky.

Thank god he can't see me, because I'm blushing so hard as soon as I hear that change in his voice.

'Oh shit, I'm sorry!' I swear I'm the ugliest shade of red. My face feels so hot.

'Absolutely nothing to be sorry for, sweetheart.'

I need a subject change and fast before I say or do something I shouldn't.

'So you like to travel?' I say in a bid to find something safe to talk about.

It works and we end up spending hours talking about travel and all the places he has been. Right up until he asks where I've travelled to.

'Ahhh I don't fly.' I laugh. 'There's no way I'm getting on a plane!'

'What? Why not? They're safer than cars.'

'When was the last time people walked away from a plane crash?'

He laughs so hard at me. 'Oh my god, girl! What is wrong with you?'

'I'm serious! No one walks away from plane crashes!' I practically shout down the phone at him.

Is he laughing harder? Why is he finding this funny?

Once he catches his breath, he manages, 'So you don't fly at all? Have you ever?'

'Yes, I have. I just don't like it and won't do it unless it's life and death!'

I'm sure he can hear how incensed I am and I swear it's making him laugh harder! Fuck!

'Life and death, you say?' he chokes out around his laughter.

'Mhm, life and death only!'

'What about for love?'

The question throws me. 'Umm, what now?'

'I'm just asking a question. Would you do it for that?' There's something in his voice that has me looking hard for the right answer.

'Ummm.' I'm struggling to answer this question. Would I fly for love? I don't even know.

'Umm is not an answer there, sweetheart.' Oh my GOD! He called me sweetheart again. My thoughts are a complete jumble.

'To be honest I've never really thought about it.' I'm struggling hard to find my footing. He has me all flustered and I can't think straight.

'Maybe you should is all I'm saying, honey.'

I have no words. I almost drop my phone with my jaw. 'I think you need to say a little more,' I manage to get out in a shaky voice.

He laughs. 'Not tonight! It's late. Say goodnight to me, Marie.'

Excuse me? He is ending the call without explanation?

'What now?' I stammer.

'Say goodnight. I'm going to bed!' Oh, he sounds cute when he is demanding.

'You wanna say goodnight, you say it.' He can hear the sass in my voice. If he wants to go, he can do it!

'Okay. Goodnight, sweetheart! I will talk to you again soon. Kiss, kiss,' Mike says without effort.

'Fine! Goodnight, Mike. I will talk to you again soon, I am sure. Love you.' I hang up and it dawns on me what I said.

Jesus, Marie! Did you just say what I think you said?! Are you insane, woman? Less than a week in and you drop 'love you'? *Ding.* I stare wide-eyed at my phone. I don't want to pick it up and see what he says. No doubt something like, 'Wow, goodbye stage five clinger.' I shake my head at myself. I said it without thinking it through. I say it to Tash every time I hang up from her – it's just what you say. *Ding.* Oh, another message. I'm going to have to look.

Did I hear what I thought I heard?

Are you going to answer me?

How the fuck does he expect me to answer that? I absently play with my hair, a nervous thing I do when unsure.

Depends, what did you hear?

Hopefully he just leaves it alone. It wasn't said in a bad way. It was habit – well, I think it was habit. I'm sticking with habit! I need Tash so bad right now. *Ding.*

I know what I heard. Question is, are you going to say it again?

Does he want me to? I'm confused.

Do you want me to?

I sit there staring at my phone waiting for the reply. What if he doesn't reply. Ugh! I'm all confused and I think I want to say it again! I know I want to hear it. *Ding.*

Goodnight, Marie! Xxoo

GOODNIGHT?? He said goodnight! Okay, I can do this.

Goodnight, Mike. Xxoo

I put my phone down and roll a smoke. I think about everything, particularly what I said. Maybe I scared him off, maybe he thinks I'm clingy, maybe I should be more careful about what I say when we are talking. I mean, right up until those words left my mouth we were getting along really well. I don't even know what to think or say to him to make it better. I finish my cigarette, leave my phone in the kitchen and go to bed. My head is a swirling mess of thoughts. Sleep will not come easy tonight.

∾ Chapter 4 ∾

The next morning, I wake up and check my phone almost as soon as I get to the kitchen. Nothing. No messages. I know he's been awake for hours. Should I message him? Say hello? Good morning? Ugh! Too many questions before coffee. I make a coffee and go to sit outside. I listen to the early morning birds waking up. It's so early. I only got a few hours of broken sleep because I couldn't turn my head off. This is not going to be a pleasant day at all. I need a plan – I focus better with a plan. Even if it's just enough to clear these thoughts for a while. I finish my coffee and go to stand up. *Ding.* The sound drops me back into my seat. I eye the phone on the table. I don't think I want to pick it up. It starts ringing and my heart flies into my throat. I lean over and look at it – Tash. Thank god!

'Hi, babe,' I say flatly.

'What's wrong?' She can tell by the tone of my voice that there's something wrong.

'Nothing, I didn't sleep well. That's all.' She's going to know there's more to it.

'Liessss! Don't you lie to me, lady! Out with it.' Damn that woman for knowing me so well.

'Okay, I was talking to Mike last night and I said something that I shouldn't have said.' I pray she just lets it drop there.

'What?'

'I said "love you" as I hung up the phone.'

She is never leaving this alone. I read his texts that followed the phone call to Tash.

'Awww, hun, I think you're overthinking it a little.' Yeah, of course I am. This is what I do – pick at it till it drives me near insane, like a scab that never heals. 'You know that the universe only sends us what we can deal with! Don't overthink it. Go get your nails done or something and get out of the house for a while.' She's right.

'You have a valid point. When are you coming to visit next?' I try for a subject change.

'I will probably come down next weekend. We need to drink and sort you out!' Oh my god, she's coming to visit! 'Now, get out of that house! Leave your phone at home and get your girly shit on! Love you, babe.'

'I love you, Tash! I'll send you pics of my nails. Laters, hun!'

She hangs up and I collect my thoughts.

She didn't even say why she had called! That woman just knows when I'm not in a good way. She always has the right words. I collect my stuff off the table, leave my phone in the kitchen and go for a shower. I find the lowest-cut top I can get my hands on, skin-tight jeans and black boots and take myself out to get my nails done.

When I finally get home after spending way too much money on clothes and other things I don't need, I put some music on and start going through the things I bought. I start dancing around the lounge while singing. I feel one hundred per cent better about everything. I'd stopped thinking about it all when I got in the car. There is absolutely no way to take what I said back and I decide that I really don't want to. It might be early but it is what it is and I can't change those feelings that are bubbling up in me. Why would I even want to? I mean, Tash would tell me that love isn't something to be scared of and to embrace it. She would yell at me for hiding how I feel about someone. If they don't feel the same, that's on them – be true to yourself.

I go back into the kitchen, dancing the whole way, pick up my phone to send Tash a picture of my nails as promised and see six messages there. All from Mike. Demonstrating massive amounts of self-restraint and not opening the texts, I take the picture and send it to Tash.

Nice nails, babe! They look amazing!

Instant reply.

I currently have six messages on my phone from Mike. I haven't looked yet. I text back to her.

LOOK!

Geez, okay!

Lord, that woman can get yell-y! I take a deep breath and steel myself for the inevitable. I just know these texts are going to be, 'It's been nice and all, but I don't think you're the *one*. Have a good life' kind of thing. Another deep breath. I open the first one.

Hola, Marie. Sorry I haven't been in touch, I was swamped at work.

Okay, so nothing bad, I read the rest and it is just a whole bunch of nothing important until the last one. I re-read it so many times and still don't think I'm getting it right. I read it slowly.

I heard what you said last night. I don't love easily, I've been burnt before. That said I would very much like to continue to get to know you. <3 Mike xxoo.

He sent me a heart! OH MY GOD! I take a screenshot of the message and send it to Tash followed by several love hearts.

See! I told you! He just needed time to realise you're amazing and it'll work out!

Work out? We are in different countries for a start of why this could end in heartbreak. We don't really know each other and I already dropped the L word – admittedly by accident, but it's out there now and you really can't just take that shit back! To be honest the more I think about it, the more I don't want to. I mean, would it have slipped out if I didn't feel that already? *Ding.*

ANSWER HIM! Get out of that overthinking head of yours. LOL.

Damn, woman knows me too well.

I'm on it. Geez!

I take a deep breath and look at his messages again. I read through them and compose myself some.

Hi, Mike. Sorry I've been out most of the morning. I got my nails done and bought some new clothes. I'm sorry about last night, it just slipped out. Anyways, I hope you're having an amazing day. Marie xo

I send the text and go out for a cigarette. I feel a little more at ease. I draw on my cigarette and contemplate what I'm going to make for dinner. I just can't do Uber again. Something homemade for sure. I walk back inside and check out the fridge but it's looking rather bare. I seriously need a personal shopper! Grocery shopping is the worst.

I move on to the freezer and find it's also rather bare. When did this happen? I really need to start eating more than once a day. I pull my vodka out of the freezer. Liquid dinner it is then. I'll shop tomorrow.

After pouring my drink I decide I'll watch a movie. Never a good thing – it'll put me to sleep for sure! I flick through the choices and settle on one after about ten minutes. I get comfy and start the movie.

Ding. The sound wakes me up. Every time! Why do I even own a TV? I pick my phone up.

Hi, honey. Just checking in before I go to bed for the night. I also wanted to say goodnight, so goodnight. Mike xxoo

Aww, a goodnight text.

Goodnight, Mike! Sleep well and I will see you tomorrow. Xxoo

I check the time – nine p.m. I go outside and roll a cigarette. How long did I sleep for? I remember the start of the movie and that seems to be it. I look back at the TV; it's long finished by the looks of it. Considering I hadn't slept well last night, I probably needed a decent catch-up nap. Although I'm not thrilled about the time of day that happened. I finish my smoke and head upstairs. Maybe a shower and bed.

Chapter 5

The months roll by. The random texts throughout the day have become wake-up texts and several every day, all day calls. Some days three or four calls. I can't get enough of this man. He's so funny, sweet and kind. He listens to me and seems genuinely interested in what is happening in my everyday life.

I walk through my front door. It's been a massive day. I just want to sit down and put my feet up and relax. I walk outside for a cigarette, look up and nearly drop my smokes.

'What are you doing here?!' I almost yell when I spot Tash sitting in front of me.

'Calm down, lady! I told you I was coming down. Remember.' She was eyeing me. 'Oh, wait maybe you forgot cause YOU HAVEN'T ANSWERED ME!' Natasha yelling was rare and a massive warning.

'I'm sure I did answer you,' I say quietly. 'I mean, when have I ever not answered you?'

She huffs at me and then stands up and hugs me so tight! 'I've missed you, sweet cheeks.' Tash is five foot of solid, southern American redneck. She has sweet blue eyes, reddish brown hair, and is covered in so many tattoos and piercings. She has a southern drawl and a heart of gold.

She squeezes a little tighter as I hug her back. I've missed Tash so much.

'Now, roll me a smoke and tell me EVERYTHING!' she says as she claps her hands and takes her seat back. As I sit down across the table from her, Tobi jumps in my lap. Of course, she brought her dog with her. If he chews my shit, I'll skin the little shit alive. Tash looks at Tobi and it's like she knows. 'Me and Tobs had a chat and he promised not to touch the expensive shoes this time.' She is dead serious and I crack up laughing at her.

I delve into the story that's me and Mike so far, telling her everything. I show her some of his pictures that he has sent through over the weeks and when she sees his dog, she falls in love with her. 'Does he know you're scared of big dogs?'

I look up at her. She can see it on my face that I haven't told him that part.

When I was three, I was attacked by a German shepherd and that is what he has. I hadn't told him that for that reason alone. 'I'll tell him if and when I need to.'

Tash laughs at me. She knows there's no reason to push the point now. 'Marie! You're so damn stubborn! I can see that set in your jaw.' She continues laughing. 'I think we need a drink if you're going to keep talking.'

Tash walks inside. She knows where everything is and she makes us drinks while I roll her and myself another smoke. I look up at the sky and can see lightning on the horizon. It's going to be a wet night. I can hear the thunder in the distance. Storms have always scared me a lot and so I'm happy Tash is here tonight to ride this one out with me.

'Here!' Tash shoves a drink at me as she sits back down. 'So where were we?' I look down at my phone and show her the picture of his dog again.

She looks at it for a second and out of the blue asks, 'So has he said it yet?'

My eyes go wide.

'Said what exactly?' I know exactly what she's asking but when she pokes something she wants all the info.

'Oh, I wonder?' She taps her chin with her forefinger. 'Has he said, "I love you" yet?'

I look her dead in the eye and she knows before the words even leave my mouth. 'No, he hasn't.' I pick up the lighter and light my cigarette.

'Oh, honey! He will. Boys are dumb like that, they just take time to work up the courage, but he'll say it! I mean, what's not to love?'

This, right here, is why I love this woman so much. She only ever sees the good and refuses to give the bad the time of day. Tash is right, I need to refocus on something other than not hearing that yet. I pet Tobi and start drinking my drink.

Tash is watching the lightning when she says, 'I think you should say it again.'

I choke on the drag I had just taken of my smoke. That woman has impeccable timing as always. 'What?!' I say, still coughing.

'You heard me. All that choking, are you practising?' She smirks at me.

I barely catch my breath from the first question only to lose it again as I cry laughing. 'Fucking what?' I stammer out, trying to breathe.

Tash has that sparkle in her eyes she gets when she's about to bombard me with all the questions most people think are too personal to ask. I down my drink and hand her the glass. 'Make it stronger if you're going to ask those questions!' I warn her.

We're both laughing still. 'I'm going to heart pour this for you and then me and you are going to get to the goods!' She walks inside.

Oh, good lord. Tash's heart pouring is basically straight vodka.

She walks back out and hands me the glass. 'I added a lime wedge. It's not completely vodka.' She laughs at me as I try it and breathe out heavily.

'Jesus, Tash! Are you trying to kill me?'

'No… but I want the goods and you always tell me more when you're drunk! So, drink up babe!'

We drink and laugh for hours when she finally decides to start asking questions. She's seen me check my phone a dozen times looking for texts from Mike. She knows I'm hooked already.

'You know he probably feels the same way you do!'

I look up at her, the two of her. She's watching me closely; anyone else would have missed it completely.

'How do you know that?' I laugh. 'Spoken to him, have you?'

I can almost hear her roll her eyes at me.

'So, sent him anything other than your face?'

I laugh a little harder. 'Not yet! Fuck it, I'mma go take a boob shot for him now!' I go to stand up and promptly sit back down. 'Tash, how much vodka is left?'

'Of yours? None... But I brought some on my way here. We are two and a half bottles in, sweet-cheeks. I wouldn't risk walking right now.' I hear her laugh, pealing bell. 'Take the pic here.'

Oh lord, I'm going to feel this in the morning... maybe the afternoon. I am going to need to sleep this off.

I pick up my phone, find the camera and take the picture. I hand my phone to Tash and ask what she thinks.

'Not bad. You can do better though.' She hands the phone back to me.

'Do better? With this much vodka in my blood stream?' I laugh. 'I'm impressed I could find the camera!' I take a few more pictures. 'I'll be right back!' I push Tobi off my lap and stumble inside.

As I come back out, I see Tash putting my phone back down.

'TASH!'

She jumps and she turns to look at me. A smile plays across her face.

'What did you do?!'

Tash starts laughing uncontrollably.

'I did nothing! Cross my heart!'

Ding.

Everything goes very quiet. I look at Tash and her face is completely neutral. A feat, considering the amount of alcohol we have drunk.

'Am I opening that?' I ask, my voice somewhere between amused and panicked.

'I wouldn't.'

I start laughing. 'I love you! I'm going to leave my phone here and go to bed. Let's go.'

Tash follows me upstairs as the storm starts to rage outside. Tash sleeps in with me, knowing the storms scare me.

The next morning, I wake up and the sun is shining brightly through the window. Tash is snoring quietly next to me. She's pant-less. Nothing unusual about that – to be honest, getting her to keep her pants on is more of a challenge. I head downstairs, leaving Tash to sleep it off and make a coffee. Heading outside for a smoke, I let Tobi out at the same time. I feel absolutely terrible. Although, considering the empty bottles on the counter, I'm surprised I'm alive. As I sit down at the table I see my phone and pick it up in hopes of a message.

There's a few messages from Mike. As I scroll to the top of the first one, I almost die! Is that my boobs? YES! I don't remember sending those. I put my head in my hands. I'm completely unsure if I should read his messages now. I sip my coffee and roll a smoke. I need painkillers to stop the pounding in my head. I walk back inside and take some painkillers. As I sit back at the table, I try to remember what happened last night. I mean, it breaks the ice a bit, I guess. I look up as Tash comes out, looking the way I feel.

'Tash, did I send my boobs last night?'

She looks up at me, wide-eyed. 'Oh shit! Did you?' She sits down next to me.

'I don't know! Here.' I hand her my phone. 'Read!'

I watch her face intently as she slowly reads the messages I couldn't bring myself to read. A slow smile spreads across her face. She puts the phone down and looks at me. 'You need to read those! But go a little higher than the picture.'

I pick up my phone. Scroll past the picture and read there first. Tash watches me this time as my eyes pop out of my head a little.

'Tash,' I whisper.

'I know right! You heart poured right in his texts!' She laughs. 'Annnnndddd then sent him boobs!' She laughs at me then clutches her head. 'We drank too much,' Tash says a little quietly.

I get up and get her some painkillers. I hand them to her with a glass of water and take my seat.

'Should I read what he said?'

Tash nods her head.

Wow! Firstly, thank you! Your words are just so sweet and well, the pic was just hot! I know I have feelings there for you, Marie. I don't love easily but I know I do love you. I guess the distance has me a little worried, but I would love to continue to get to know you and see how things go from there.

Call me when you wake up?

I smile stupidly at my phone, my heart full.

'We need food! I'm ordering pizza.' Tash's talking pulls me out of my head. 'Food and movie day! Let's go!'

Chapter 6

Tash stayed for a week and it was amazing having her here for that time. I didn't realise how much I'd missed having her around until I came home from work and she'd vanished. There was a note on the counter.

It's been amazing spending the last week with you! I must get back to my things and stuffs! I love you, lady, never ever forget that!! Call me on the weekend! Love you!!!

I wasn't happy about her leaving but this was Tash and this woman has been my rock for years! I wouldn't dare change her from who she is.

My phone rings. I look at it and my heart skips a beat. It's Mike.

'Hello, honey,' I answer the phone.

'Hi, sweetheart.' I will never get sick of hearing that. 'It's been a while! How have you been?'

'Sorry, I've missed hearing your voice, to be honest! I felt like I was missing something important all week and I couldn't place it until right now!' Well, that was honest.

'Aww, that's sweet. I've missed you too but wanted to give you time with your friend... It kind of sucked if I'm completely honest.' He sounded genuine.

'I had a blast with Tash. She is my rock after all.' I laugh, remembering some of what happened.

'I'm glad you had a good time, honey! You probably needed it.' He sounds so happy. It makes me tingle in places it definitely shouldn't.

'The first night I swear she was trying to kill me! Almost three bottles of vodka!' I laugh and he laughs with me, the sound making those tingling spots throb.

I make a slight sound, almost a moan – different to what he is used to hearing.

'Well, that is the sweetest sound I've heard in a long time.' His voice is husky, a little charming. Just the change in his voice is making me wet.

'Was it just?' I ask quietly.

'Absolutely! I could listen to that all day long!' His voice has changed again – damn it's sexy. Another slight moan escapes me. 'Mmm, woman!'

I laugh, a little husky myself. 'I think I'm going to take you to the bedroom,' I say softly.

I can hear him breathing but he doesn't say a word.

'Would you like that?' I ask as I make my way to the bedroom door. I pause, waiting for the answer.

He takes a deep breath. 'I think so. Take me to bed.'

That was all I needed to push me through the doorway and into the bedroom. Taking my pants off, I make my way to the bed. I run a finger over my clit, a moan escaping my lips.

'Jesus, that's hot.' He breathes into the phone.

I rub my clit a little more, the sound of his voice triggering something deep inside of me. I moan louder while letting out the breath I've been holding. 'Do you want to hear me cum?' I whisper into the phone.

'You have no idea how much!' His voice is deep and full of want. The sound drives my fingers into my wetness, my moans coming louder.

I draw my fingers back to my aching clit and rub it a little as my breathing gets heavier and I gasp a little. I can hear his breathing change as well, giving the impression that he is doing what I am doing. Just the thought gives me goosebumps and makes my clit pulse. I reach over to my bedside drawer and grab my vibrator. The second it hits my clit I moan loudly.

'Yes, baby girl,' he breathes heavily into the phone.

I turn the vibrator up and arch my back, my breathing quicker, gasping and moaning the whole time.

'Ooooh my god.' I exhale. I can feel an orgasm building. What I would give to feel his hands on my hips right now, pulling me onto his cock. Just the thought is enough to push me over that edge. I cum, panting as I try to catch my breath.

I lay on my bed breathing, happy and somewhat sated. I can hear him breathing hard too. 'How you going over there?' I ask, my voice quiet, almost sweet.

'Jesus, Marie! That was so sexy.' He sounds breathless.

I giggle a little, suddenly feeling a little embarrassed. 'Please tell me you aren't going to disappear tomorrow!' I joke.

'Are you kidding me?' He laughs. 'You are amazing!'

I blush at his words and suddenly feel a little shy.

'I wish I was there making you make those sounds!'

I huff out a breath. 'I don't know what to say.'

He must hear the uncertainty in my voice.

'Marie?' He waits for a response from me and I mumble one. 'I love you and thank you.'

I'm completely dumbfounded and speechless. Did I just hear those words I've been waiting for for weeks?

'Baby? Are you okay?' He sounds concerned.

'I-I'm… okay… I-I-I'm a little speechless, Mike,' I stutter.

He laughs at me, and we continue talking for hours about our week and various other little topics. I hear him yawn. It must be the third or fourth time in the last ten minutes.

'Time to say it, hun,' I say quietly.

'No, I don't want to. I'm okay.' He muffles another yawn as I look at the clock. It's almost midnight. It has to be nearly four a.m. there.

'Goodnight, Mike,' I say determinedly.

'Fine.' He huffs at me.

'No, no. That's not how this works. I'm home all day tomorrow. I will call you when I wake up. We can talk all day if you want.'

I can hear him yawn again. 'Okay, sweetheart. I love you. Sleep well and we will talk in the morning.' Oh my goodness, he said it again!

'I love you too, Mike. I will let you know when I'm awake. Goodnight!'

'Goodnight, Marie.' And he was gone.

I lay on my bed thinking about the whole call. I have never been like that on the phone. For weeks there has been sexual tension between us, but it had never progressed past teasing and desire. I need to text Tash! I pick my phone up and send her a text.

OMG I'm a total hoe! But he said those words!! I'll call you later. Goodnight xxoo

Chapter 7

I wake up to a text from Tash and one from Mike. I read Tash's first and answer hers with all the details of what had happened the night before. Thinking back on it this morning, it makes me smile. It wasn't planned and it was so damn hot. I need to figure out how to get that man's hands on this body and soon. I know I need him in my life and in so many ways.

I roll out of bed and go for a shower. I can't stop thinking about the phone call from last night; it's a massive turn-on. I can feel the ache between my thighs – add to that the absolute bliss of the warm water running over my body and I'm horny again. I start to rub my clit in tight little circles when I hear my phone ringing. I huff out a breath. It's like people know I'm touching it! UGH. I get out of the shower and answer my phone.

'Hello, gorgeous!' Tash has amazing timing as always.

'Morning, Tash. You're calling rather early.' I wonder if she can hear the frustration in my voice. Maybe it's just something I was feeling instead.

'For someone who hoed it up last night, you seem a little testy! Need to rub another one out, babe?'

I laugh at her. That woman just knows.

'You kinda interrupted me, if I'm honest. I was in the shower.'

'Ooooh, Mr Showerhead about to get a workout? Either way, we are going to have a chat first and then I will let you get back to the showerhead because lord knows I love mine!'

I laugh at her as I sit on the bed slowly drying off.

Tash and I speak for a few hours. She got home to a mess and needed to vent and get it all out. I feel for her; life is hard sometimes, but she is getting it sorted and said she may come back for a visit soon. When we finally get off the phone, she sounds happier and more grounded.

I walk into the kitchen and make another coffee. I should probably eat something too. I go about making food and go and sit outside in the warmth to eat. I pick up my phone and read the text from Mike again.

Good morning, sweetheart! I really enjoyed our call last night and not just 'that part' either! The whole thing. You are amazing and I really like my time with you. I love you, Marie. I hope to talk to you soon. Call me when you wake up.

I finish eating and make the call as requested.

'Good morning, sweetheart!'

Oh, the way he answered the call made me feel so loved.

'Good morning! How are you today?'

'I haven't been able to stop thinking about you is how I am. I wish we were closer, to be honest. I want, no need, to be the one making you make those sounds. I want to see it, feel it and hear it!' His voice is husky, making me ache and throb again. Damn, that man is hot!

'Mmmm, that would be amazing! I wish we could have that, Mike, so much!' I wonder if he can hear the want I'm feeling in this moment.

'Why can't we? I mean, the ocean and distance aren't that bad. Maybe we can plan something.'

Oh shit, have I told him I am scared of flying? I'm sure I have mentioned it before...

'Well, there's that flying thing...' I trail off.

'Yes, I remember you saying. I'm worth it though.' Of course he is but this is a massive fear of mine. I also don't want to disappoint him.

'So, what's on the agenda today?' I try for a subject change.

'I think we need to talk about this flying thing first. I would love to see you, hold you, be with you! That's kind of impossible with an ocean and your fear holding you back.' He needs to stop poking this right now. Fears are irrational, I know this, but talking about it right now isn't going to change it and will only end in a fight!

'I understand you'd like to talk about it, but today isn't the day. So, let's move on to something else.'

He can hear the warning in my voice and completely ignores it.

'Okay, well, I have stuff to do. Call me later if you wanna talk about this. Love you.' And he was gone!

Did he just hang up on me? Over a fear? A legitimate fear at that! It's not like I'm the only person in the world scared of flying! UGH, men! I continue silently raging in my head. I slam my phone down on the table, stand up and walk inside. I pick up my keys and walk out the front door. I need some fresh air and I need to sit by the water to clear my head. If he thinks I'm going to call him back anytime soon, he is dreaming!

I get to my destination, park my car and walk down to the water. I sit down on the sand and listen to the waves crashing onto the shore, promptly bursting into tears. The beach is pretty with its golden sands and blue water. Off to the left are rock pools that I used to explore as a kid and to the right are cliff faces, dark grey with seagulls nesting along the face. I remember base jumping off them as a teenager.

I haven't been this torn up over someone in years. Where are all these feelings coming from? I've been in relationships before and never felt like this. I've never felt like my heart had been ripped out of my chest before. How do you feel something like that for a man that you've only spoken to over the phone and seen photos of? Admittedly, we speak every day for hours, sharing everything. He knows so much about me that most don't. I think he even knows things that Tash doesn't, and that woman is basically my sister in every way but blood and name. I cry a little harder; it feels like I'm losing something that I'm not prepared to lose.

This man has become so much more to me than I ever expected. I mean we met on a dating site! We are an ocean apart! I look out over the ocean – in the general direction he would be – and I suddenly wonder if he is feeling the same way? Why didn't he just let it go?

I know why he didn't, why he couldn't leave it alone – he wants me in his arms just as much as I want to be in them. Wrapped up, being able to smell him, feel him, experiencing that unique safe feeling that comes with being with someone who loves you. I cry again.

I sit there for hours, overthinking everything. I just can't seem to turn it all off. I'm watching a storm roll in off the coast and it is getting closer, like the universe can feel my inner turmoil and the storm is the end result of it, a way to cleanse the thoughts. I sit watching it a little longer. As it starts to rain, I feel something change. I get up and walk back to my car. I'm soaked by the time I get to it. I'm sitting in the empty parking lot, listening to the thunder crash around me and for the first time in a long time, I'm not scared. The realisation shocks me. I start my car and drive home as fast as I safely can.

As soon as I walk into the house, I get changed and warm up a little. I look everywhere for my phone. I have a call to make! Where did I leave it? I hear the thunder in the distance, and it dawns on me that I left it outside on the table. I race outside to get it. Picking it up, I see there is a message from Mike. It was sent almost four hours ago. How long was I gone? I look up at the sky. It's getting late. I open the message.

Hi, honey. I hope you're okay? I am sorry for hanging up on you.

Short and to the point. Man of few words when he doesn't know how it will be received and, considering it's now been four hours since he sent it, he probably thinks I'm ignoring him. I sit down and roll a smoke. My head has settled some since the initial anger and upset I first felt. Now all I want is to hear his voice and make sure he is okay!

Hello, Mike. Sorry for the delay in answering. I was out and left my phone at home... on purpose. I'm going to make something to eat 'cos I haven't eaten a lot today and I might call you after if you want.

I deliberately left emotion out of my reply. I'm still raw from all the emotions coursing through me and I'm feeling a little exposed. I go to make something to eat. I put some music on and cook.

Ding. The sound makes my heart pound. I stop dancing in my kitchen and look over at the table where my phone is sitting. I walk over slowly and look down at my phone. My heart is feeling like it's going to burst out of my chest. I pick up my phone and open the message.

Why haven't you eaten? And yes, please call me after you eat.

Do I answer him? Or just leave it until I call him? I think about it for a few minutes and decide I'll answer him.

I was out and wasn't hungry. I'm cooking at the moment, I'll let you know when I'm going to call.

I put my phone down, turn my music up loud and continue cooking so it's not surprising I miss the next message.

Okay baby, I love you.

After I eat my dinner, I see his message finally and it melts me a little. I didn't realise I'd been holding onto the cold that had swept over me earlier today. Self-preservation: stop feeling and it stops hurting. It's something I've been able to do since I was a child. I was good at turning everything off and not feeling it so I can do the normal people things. It has always been a struggle to turn them back on, but those words from him had me feeling again within seconds. To be honest it was like a punch in the stomach, knocking the wind right out of my sails.

Are you okay if I call now?

My phone rings in my hand, throwing me a little as I was expecting a text back.

'Hey,' I answer the phone.

'Hi, babe.' He sounds like I feel. I am instantly lost for words. He is hurting too. I don't know how to process this kind of information this fast. 'You're quiet.'

'Sorry.' It's all I can say without my voice cracking and crying.

'No need to be sorry, honey. What did you have for dinner?' The change in subject throws me a little more.

'Umm, just a chicken salad wrap. Are you okay, Mike?' I need to know he's okay.

'Getting better by the minute, baby girl.' My heart soars hearing those words.

The conversation starts to flow a little easier after that. We spend hours on the phone talking about everything and anything. I don't tell him what I felt while I was out 'collecting my thoughts'. For some reason, I feel like it would scare him away. So I hide it from him. Something I might come to regret a little later, but right now I feel like I need to. He makes sure I am in bed before he hangs up.

Once I hang up from Mike, I call Tash.

'Hello, sweets. What do I owe the pleasure at this time of night?' Tash sounds busy.

'I need your help with something. I have an idea and I can't do it alone,' I say sleepily.

'Oooooh, tell me everything and I'll make it happen!'

I start telling Tash my idea and what I need to make it happen. Tash listens intently and gives me suggestions to speed things up. It is going to take time but between us we can make this work.

Chapter 8

The weeks roll into months, and everything seems good between me and Mike. We laugh and speak daily. I've been making plans with Tash to go visit for a week or two. She is currently in the city and her company paid for the penthouse! Who would say no to that?! Natasha has also been helping me make other plans considering it is coming up to Mike's birthday and there is something I want to get him. Something special.

'So how did you go?' I ask Tash as I walk into the penthouse and my jaw hits the ground. 'Holy shit! This place is amazing!'

Tash laughs. 'Right! I could see me living here permanently.' She walks over to me and squeezes me in a bear hug that is uniquely Natasha. 'Yes, it's all sorted. Are you going to be able to do it?' I can hear the concern in her voice.

'Remember how scared of storms I am?' I ask, walking further into the penthouse apartment and putting my stuff down in the lounge.

'Yep, I remember,' she says, following me into the massive kitchen.

'Yeah, well, they don't scare me anymore.'

Tash stops what she's doing and looks at me.

'Remember when we had that fight a few months back and I spent the better part of a day at the beach watching that storm roll in?'

She nods her head.

'Well, I didn't leave the beach till it hit. I wasn't scared at all, sitting in it, driving in it – none of it scared me.'

Tash looks thoughtful.

'Well, hopefully it will help! You've got this.' She hugs me again. She's excited; she wants this for me.

We sit and talk for a while and she explains what's going to happen. She knows I'm terrified about what's coming but she also knows I'm ready for this and need that push. Tash has done an amazing job organising everything for me.

'Are you okay, Marie?' Tash watches me walk past her for the tenth time.

'Mhm, I'm fine.' I turn and walk back across the room again.

'Good lord, woman! SIT!' Tash grabs my arm as I walk past and forces me into the seat next to her. 'Take a deep breath! Everything will be okay, I promise, babe!'

I look at her and she can see I'm far from fine. 'I need a drink… a strong one.'

'Stay right there, I will get it for you! DON'T MOVE,' she growls at me as she walks into the kitchen. She is back within a minute. 'Here, shot first and then drink this.' She hands me a shot. I nearly choke on it – tequila. I should have known. She shoves a vodka and soda into my hand. 'Drink it! You need to chill out a little or you're going to make yourself sick.'

After coughing through the shot, I drink the vodka. 'Are you trying to kill me again, Tash?!' I cough again. Tash laughs as I continue to sip the drink. My phone rings.

I nearly drop my glass. It's his ring – I changed it a while back, so I knew when Mike was calling me. 'I can't answer that, Tash! I can't talk to him!'

She can hear the panic in my voice.

She picks up my phone. 'Hello, Marie's phone, Natasha speaking.' She is smiling and nodding her head to whatever is being said on the other end of my phone call. 'Yes, of course I will let her know.' She stops and listens again. 'Don't worry, I will pass the message on for you. Okay, goodbye.'

I look at her nervously. 'I feel so bad, Tash. He probably doesn't understand at all.' She can see the tears I refuse to let fall.

'Honey.' She kneels down in front of me and takes my head in her hands. 'You're doing the right thing. I promise everything will be perfect.' She sees me starting to cry. Tash leans forward and wraps her arms around me.

'I just want to hear his voice, Tash,' I sob out and she hugs me harder. The only reason I haven't spoken to him in the last few days is because I knew I'd give away his birthday surprise.

'Marie, go have a smoke on the balcony, take your drink and get some fresh air. You just need to clear your head a little. Everything will be okay.' She stands me up and gives me a slight push towards the door, taking my phone with her, which earned her my best glare. 'Taking temptation away, that's all. You need your space at the moment.'

I walk outside and the tears continue to fall. Will he ever forgive me? This is the hardest thing I've ever done and hopefully he understands one day that what I did, I did for him. I haven't spoken to him for a week while everything was being planned – I put off calls, avoided texts and only answered minimal times. The man was lucky to get one text a day! But talking to him, I would have spilled my guts and he'd know I'd sold my house, car and everything to throw life in his direction. I walk over to the balustrade and look out over the city. It's so pretty and yet feels so cold. All those people down there that have what I don't have, feeling all the things with their loved one that I can't. Being wrapped up in the arms of the person who completes them, fighting with the person who tests them, making love to the person who just knows how to do that thing that tips them over and riding that wave with them.

I finish my drink and can feel my head spinning. Tash knows how to turn the emotions off in a hurry. I feel sad and exhausted. I walk back inside and tell Tash I'm going to bed.

I take my clothes off and fall into bed naked. I can't shake the feeling that Mike is suffering, not knowing what I know. I just hope he can wait out the heart ache for just a little while. I close my eyes… I dream.

I walk into a house that isn't familiar to me. I swear it's Mike's voice that I can hear. I walk further into the house and find him sitting in a lounge. The TV is on, but he seems to have it on for the noise more than anything else. He hasn't seen me yet. I walk a little further forward.

'Mike?' I say quietly.

He turns to look at me. He holds that look for a long minute and before I can say another word, he moves. He wraps his arms around me and kisses me with so much passion and love that it takes my breath away. Without skipping a beat, he starts taking my clothes off as he slowly pushes me back towards the couch, kissing me the whole time. I fall onto the couch, and he is right there with me. I can feel his skin on mine; I can smell him, taste him on my lips. I moan as he kisses my neck, slowly working down my body, licking and sucking my nipples till they're hard, my hands in his hair. My breathing increases the closer he gets to my pussy. I can feel nothing but tingling and throbbing in anticipation of feeling his tongue slide into me and his lips wrapping around my clit. As soon as I feel those lips, I arch my pussy into his mouth, demanding more. I feel his hands holding onto my ass, pulling me in closer to his mouth. His tongue teases me closer and closer with every flick. He is listening to my breathing getting faster, my moaning getting louder and just as I'm about to cum, he locks his lips around my clit and sucks. I scream out an orgasm, gasping...

I wake up. I'm hot, sweaty and fucking horny! I look out the window and see the sun is just starting to peak out over the horizon. It's early. After that dream, there is no way I'm getting back to sleep. I feel a pang of guilt as I remember the dream. I miss Mike, so much. I roll onto my back and stare at the ceiling. That man is in my head... Who am I kidding? That man is a part of my soul. The missing piece of it. A tear falls onto the pillow. I sigh and get out of bed. I walk into the ensuite and have a hot shower. Today is going to be hard enough without getting caught up in my head. I take a few deep breaths and mentally prepare for the challenges I'm about to face alone.

Tash hugs me goodbye as I get out of the cab. 'You're going to be fine, babe! I will call you later, okay!' She kisses my cheek hard and is trying not to cry. I turn and walk into the building. I take a deep breath, praying to anyone listening that I'm doing the right thing.

❧ *Chapter 9* ❧

I take a seat and wait. I can feel the nerves building in me. I look at the door and know it would be so easy just to walk out and run away from all of this. I swallow hard and take a deep breath. I know there's no turning back. Everything I've done in the last month was for this end goal.

'*Now boarding flight 434 to Bora Bora at terminal 16.*' The announcement pulls me out of my head and back into reality. I stand up and make my way to the terminal.

I can do this. I close my eyes and take a deep breath as I walk down the gangway towards the plane. I am absolutely shitting myself at this point, but every step brings me that much closer to being in his arms.

I enter the plane and find my seat. I am sitting next an older lady. She smiles at me and suddenly I don't feel as nervous. She's small with kind eyes and a pink streak in the front of her hair. Her face shows the wrinkles of a person who has spent the days of her youth laughing and happy.

'Hello, darling,' she says to me. 'You look like you've seen a ghost. Are you okay?'

I smile at her very accurate description of my face right now.

'No, not really! Flying scares the shit out of me!' I half-laugh and half-choke a sob back.

She pats the seat next to her. 'Sit, you can hold my hand if you're scared. If you don't mind me asking though, why are you flying if it scares you so much?' Old people, always so nosy.

'The man I love is on the other side of this ocean and I have waited long enough to see him.' My voice cracks slightly; I'm not sure if it's the flying or that I'm actually going to see him.

'I'm sure he is excited that you're coming. My name is Elsie.' She introduces herself.

I tell her my name. 'He might be if he knew I was coming. It's a surprise. For his birthday.' I take a deep breath as the engines start to warm up. I grip the arm rests.

Elsie takes my hand. 'Tell me about him?' she asks.

I look at her and start telling her about Mike. What he looks like with his green eyes and five days of growth on his face. I tell her about the cutest little creases around his eyes when he laughs, what his voice sounds like, the way he makes me feel as soon as I see he is calling or texting me. I get so caught up talking about Mike that I miss the take off and don't realise we are airborne until the air hostess asks if we want a drink. I order two vodkas straight up. Elsie laughs.

'She's a nervous flyer,' she says when the stewardess eyes me after my order.

Elsie turns out to be funny and has no problem keeping me distracted throughout the whole flight, even making sure I am laughing hard while we are landing, telling me about a time she and her long-dead husband fought and he'd thrown his keys in a rage and then spent four hours searching for them in long grass while she sat on the veranda in the shade, sipping a drink and laughing at him the whole time.

The plane taxis to the terminal and I let out my pent-up breath. I think I've been holding it since I walked into the airport in Australia, after saying goodbye to Tash. I make my way down to the baggage collection area. I pull out my phone; there's a message from Tash.

Hi, sweet cheeks! You should be there by now. I know you were freaking out; hopefully Elsie made the flight better for you! Yes, I think of everything. Love you, lady!!

Well, Jesus, Tash is beyond amazing. She gave me an inflight fluffer!

Hi, gorgeous! I made it just fine. Elsie is funny, where did you find her? It doesn't matter!! Thank you!! I love you, lady!

I see my bag and walk forward to grab it. As I turn around, I hear, 'Want me to take that for you?'

That voice!

I look up as I half drop my bag. He grabs it and places it on the ground. My jaw hits the ground.

'Hi, sweetheart.'

I have no words and he can tell. He steps forward and before I know it, I am wrapped in those arms. He kisses the top of my head.

'How?' I murmur into his chest.

'Tash called me last week and explained what you had done and what you were planning. This last week has been a nightmare, Marie.' He sounds so happy and slightly annoyed. I don't want to look up, move or anything just in case I'm still dreaming and haven't woken up yet.

For the last month, I had sold pretty much everything I owned – my house, furniture, quit my job, left everything I had – to chase this love, my other half, the spark that was missing in my life, the other part of my soul to make it complete. It was the hardest thing I had ever done in my life. Completely worth the feeling I have right in this moment.

'Wanna go home?' Mike's voice pulls me back to the present.

'I really do, but first there's something else I really want.' I tilt my head up slightly and he looks into my eyes, places both hands on either side of my face and kisses me with everything he is. I melt into it, completely lost in that moment. He pulls back a little and I stumble forward, completely dizzy, forgetting where I am. The noise of the airport slowly creeps back into my reality.

'Come on, baby girl, let's go home.' Mike picks up my suitcase with one hand, wraps the other around my waist and we walk out to his truck. 'You're going to need to call Tash when we get there. She made me promise.' He did not sound happy about that. It made me look over at him.

'Okay... And this is an issue?' I'm confused and unsure why that would make him unhappy.

'It's not an issue as much as I'm not sure I want to share you with anyone right now.' He laughs; my heart skips a beat hearing his words and laugh.

I grin at him. 'How long before we get there?'

'About fifteen minutes... Why?'

I pull my phone out and call Tash. 'Hi, babe! Remind me to kick your ass when I see you next!'

Her laughter coming down the phone at me is amazing.

'There she is! How was the flight, oh wait… How was that first kiss?'

I laugh.

'He can hear you!' I side-eye Mike.

'Hi, Tash,' he says as he's driving.

'I don't care, I need the details! Ahhh, it doesn't matter. Don't do anything I wouldn't do! Love you, lady. Bye.' And she's gone. I laugh.

I spend the rest of the trip watching the scenery rushing past my window, somewhat in a daze. I want to pinch myself; it doesn't feel real at all. I think about all the things I hid from him over the last few months. God, I hope he doesn't hold grudges. I ignored calls, avoided questions, spent minimal time on the phone to prevent me spilling the beans to him. He must have felt like I was leaving him, the slow ghost. I look over at him.

'I'm sorry about the last month, Mike,' I say quietly.

He slows the truck to turn and looks over at me. 'Nothing to be sorry for, baby.' There's something in his voice that makes me look at him directly. 'When Tash called me and explained what was going on and why you'd been distant, I had no choice but to completely forgive you for the past month.' He took a deep breath, his hand reaching out to mine. 'I won't lie to you, I was hurt, but that little bit of hurt was completely worth what I feel now.'

I have tears and he can see it.

'Don't cry, sweetheart, everything worked out.'

I nod my head, suddenly lost for words. He pulls into a driveway. 'Honey, we're home.' He grins at me, and I laugh.

We get out of the truck and his dog Susie comes over to sniff me. I instantly stiffen up and Mike calls her to him. 'You'll get used to her. She's a big puppy.'

I smile but god, big dogs scare me almost as much as flying! He opens the front door, and we walk inside.

'Welcome home, babe.'

Chapter 10

There we are, finally close enough to touch, yet we don't. We are talking, mostly just random stuff, but it's safe. We are having a few drinks because Lord knows I need to take the edge off, but there is still space between us – too much space. To be honest, it feels like there's a whole ocean there, still, separating us. It kind of sucks but I am close enough to finally smell him, see him, watch his eyes when he looks at me, see that shyness he always claimed to have. I'm happy, I'm with my guy.

The night continues and we get more comfortable. We laugh, joke around, drink a little more and start getting flirty. Mike stands up to go get ice.

'Could you get me some too, please?'

He looks over his shoulder at me and grins.

'Something wrong with your legs, hun?'

I laugh at him and stand up. I'll go with him – it's not like I want to be anywhere he's not.

As we are getting ice, I brush past him, more to get out of his way than anything else. He makes 'that' sound, the one I've heard so many times over the phone. My heart jumps. I can feel him; he's right there, not touching me but wanting to. I take a deep breath, exhaling.

'You okay?' I ask but haven't actually looked at him. I feel like he hasn't taken his eyes off me since I brushed past him.

'You're not close enough.' He speaks so quietly that I strain a little to hear what I thought I heard.

'Did you get ice?' I know he hasn't moved; there's so much tension in that small space. I think I'm holding my breath. I need to breathe!

'No, not yet.'

I turn slightly towards him but don't make eye contact. I'm so nervous; I want to kiss and touch him so much but can't seem to make my body move! Ugh! I was right, his eyes are locked on me, almost like he wants to devour me. I seriously feel like a deer caught in headlights. Any sudden moves would give me what I want, his lips on mine. Do you think I could move?!

'Get your ice, Mike.' I'm trying hard to hold onto my equilibrium. I mean, if he wanted to, he would have kissed me by now, right?

'No... I'm good right here.' There's something a little different to his voice, different enough that I look up.

As soon as our eyes lock, he moves. He takes the glass out of my hand, placing it on the counter, while at the same time his other hand is around my waist. Just as he is about to kiss me, there's a noise. Susie knocked something over. He steps back, turning back to get his ice. We go back to the lounge.

My heart is pounding. I try hard to pour a strong-ass drink but as soon as I pick the bottle up, I can see my hand shaking. I'm dead sure he's seen it too!

'I'll be right back.' I turn and walk out of the room without waiting for a response.

Where the hell is the bathroom in this place? I try three different doors before I finally find it. I walk in, turn the light on and lock the door behind me. I stand at the sink, taking a few deep breaths. So close and yet so far! I look at myself in the mirror. My cheeks are flushed, I have butterflies and I'm a ball of nerves. I know I need to go back. I've been gone a little while, maybe five to ten minutes. I've managed to give myself a little time to kill that shaking in my hands and get my breathing and heartbeat back to a normal rhythm. I unlock the door, turn the light off and walk straight into Mike.

'Jesus! What are you doing here?' I half laugh but he has me straight back to nervous.

'Finishing what I started, sweetheart.' His hands cup either side of my face and he kisses me. I literally melt into it. As he feels the tension leave my body, he wraps me up in his arms and kisses me more deeply. I'm his and he knows it. I don't remember how long the kiss lasts because the next thing I know I'm sitting in my seat, trying to roll a smoke with shaking hands.

'Listen, Linda!'

I look up and Mike is scowling at me. Clearly I missed something.

'Sorry, I'm a little all over the place. What did you ask?'

He laughs at me.

'Jesus, woman! Are you even able to roll that right now? Did you want one of mine?'

Okay so I'd been trying to roll said smoke for a little while.

'Nah, I've got it.' I concentrate hard on what I'm doing and finally get it done. I look around for the lighter; I see it, it's in his hand.

'Can I have that, please?' Was that even my voice? Lord, I think I whispered it.

He turns his head to the side and looks at me, smiling. 'Pardon?'

I blush instantly. Damn it, he knows what he's doing.

I clear my throat and repeat, 'Can I have that please?' There's a bit of steel in it this time. He hands the lighter over to me and as soon as his hand touches mine, I drop the damn thing. I swear under my breath as I get up to get it. Mike stands at the same time. My heart is pounding; he's so close to me. I want to feel him kiss me again. I want sooo much more than that, but I'd settle for his lips pressed on mine right now.

'Hun, take a breath, relax.' He hands my drink to me, making sure I'm holding it before he lets it go. I down the whole thing.

'I need ice, I'll be back.'

'Okay, baby.' He has that playful tone. He knows damn well that he's messing with me, and I think he's enjoying it.

When I get back, he's grinning at me.

'What?'

He smiles a little wider. 'Nothing, baby girl.'

I blush again. 'Knock it off!'

Mike laughs so hard. I pour my drink and I know he is watching me. It's stronger than the last one.

'Are you okay, babyyyyy?'

I hadn't heard him get up. I didn't realise he was right behind me, so when I turned to tell him to shhhh again, I wasn't expecting to be staring him straight in the eyes. I gasp. He wraps me up in his arms and kisses me, deep, long, taking my breath away. I stumble a little when he releases me. He leaves a hand on my shoulder to steady me. I sink into my chair.

'I love you, Marie.' The words bring tears to my eyes. I drop my head a little so he can't see.

'I love you, Mike.'

He can hear I sound choked up. His girl is feeling it in that moment. I've been waiting for this for a long time – that and the massive amounts of vodka I've drunk. He takes my hand and starts to lead me from the room.

'Time for bed, honey.' He turns me towards the door and guides me to where I'm sleeping.

'But we didn't finish,' I weakly protest.

'We can finish it tomorrow.' He pushes me through the door gently and helps me into bed.

'Stay with me,' I whisper.

'Move over then. This is my side.'

I roll over and feel him slide in next to me. He pulls me close, hugging me tight in his arms and kisses the top of my head.

'Sleep, baby girl,' he whispers and I am out.

ꙵꙴ *Chapter 11* ꙴꙵ

The next morning I wake up and he's gone, quite possibly from my snoring! I lay there for a minute remembering what his lips felt like on mine. I chew on my bottom lip just at the thought. I need a shower. I get out of bed and find my stuff, get my shampoo and everything I think I need, mostly. I'm still a little dazed at being here. I head into the bathroom, looking in the mirror as I do. I look terrible! I jump in the shower and zone out as I do my thing and wash my hair. When I get out, I realise I've left all my clothes in the bedroom! I dry off a little, wrapping the towel around me and tying it in a knot so it stays where I want it. Opening the door, I head back into the bedroom. My head in my phone, laughing at Tash's comments and answering her, I'm completely oblivious to my surroundings, so I don't see him standing in the doorway. I head over to my suitcase, trying to figure out what I want to wear and trying to text Tash back at the same time.

'Good morning, honey.'

I jump and spin around, remembering rather abruptly I'm wearing a towel.

'Morning,' I stammer. He must hear the surprise in my voice.

'I've got coffee for you.'

I see the mug in his hand, but his eyes haven't left my body.

'Awww, thanks! I need coffee and drugs! How much did I drink?'

A small smile plays across Mike's face, his perfect white teeth flashing at me, his green eyes sparkling, as a deep chuckle escapes his chest.

'A lot!' he says, stepping into the room.

I freeze to the spot. He closes the door. My heart jumps into my throat. He moves closer to where I am, placing the coffee mug on the bedside as he comes towards me.

'You weren't here when I woke up,' I say quietly. My phone buzzes in my hand and I look down. When I look back up a few seconds later, Mike is right in front of me.

'I went to make my girl coffee.'

My girl. Those two words, there's no explaining how they make me feel but it's instant, spreading right through me and I want to hold onto that feeling forever. I look up at him and he steps closer.

I'm in his arms almost instantly. He kisses me. It feels different this time, intense, full of passion and want, his hands deftly undoing the knot I have tied in the towel to keep it in place. His hands are on my body the second the towel drops to the floor. He starts slowly walking me backwards towards the bed, one hand in my wet hair and the other on my pussy, his finger slipping into my wetness, making me gasp, breaking the kiss. I lift his shirt up and he stops kissing me to take it off, his pants following shortly after.

The bed is right behind me. He kisses my neck and I moan. He pushes me just enough so I fall onto the bed. I hardly land before he's on top of me, kissing me again. I can barely catch my breath as sensation spreads through my body.

He leisurely makes his way up my body, kissing me all over on his way back to my lips, making me gasp and moan softly, kissing my lips briefly before intentionally working his way back down, running his tongue over one thigh and then the other. I moan and squirm a little when he finds the spots that tickles but feels oh so good, just above my hip bone. His tongue finally finds my clit. I gasp, arching into his mouth, wanting more. I feel his hands grip my lower back, pulling me in closer. I start grinding on his face as I get closer and closer, my hand pulling his head in harder as he wraps his lips around my clit and I cum, half sitting up when I do. He pushes me back down, leaving his hand on my chest, while he continues eating me out. I cry out with another orgasm, breathing heavily.

I'm still panting when he stands up and pushes me up the bed. I feel Mike's cock slide into me, and I raise my hips to meet his. His lips find mine, kissing me while he moves in me. He has one hand on my breast, massaging and teasing the nipple to harden.

Mike listens to my moans and as I get closer, he rolls us over. I sit up and ride his glorious cock, grinding and bouncing, his hands full of my breasts. He leans forward and sucks my nipple into his mouth, teasing it with his tongue, the sensation making me grind down on him faster. His hands move to my hips pulling me down harder on his cock. I grab his head and push it harder onto my nipple. I start cumming and his grip on my hips tightens. I collapse into him a little; he moves my hips, causing me to moan in his ear.

'Cum again, baby,' he whispers to me as I start grinding harder and faster, his grip getting tighter as I cum again and he thrusts his hips forward, cumming with me. I collapse in a heap on the bed, breathing hard.

'I'm going to need another shower… Coming with me this time?' I breathe in his general direction, my eyes closed.

I lay there for a while longer, my head on his shoulder, listening to him catching his breath, hearing his heart beating in his chest. One of his hands absently traces my spine while the other rests on his stomach. I snuggle in a little closer and kiss his cheek. He turns his head towards me and kisses my forehead.

He rolls on his side, dumping me on the bed and looks at me, brushing some hair from my face with his fingers. He cups my chin, pulling my head up so I'm looking him in the eyes.

'How are those nerves now, baby girl?'

I laugh.

'Mostly gone,' I reply as he leans in and kisses me, slow and long.

'Time for a shower, baby,' Mike tells me, pulling back a little bit.

I slowly open my eyes and bite my lip. When he sees me do that, he kisses me again, biting my lip with his teeth as he pulls back.

I moan and he leans over me, looking down at me. 'Move your ass, woman!' Growling at me, I giggle and roll over, sitting up. Mike gets off the bed, taking my hands. He leads me into the bathroom. As we walk in there, I slide my hands around his waist and press up close to his back, enjoying the feel of my skin on his. I hear the shower start. He turns in my grip and pulls me into the shower.

He pushes me up against the shower wall, kissing me, his hand making its way down my side, across my stomach and sliding down to my pussy, gently rubbing my clit, making me moan into his mouth while he's kissing me.

Mike presses his body into mine harder and slides two of his fingers into me.

'Ooooh god, babe.' I gasp as he starts fucking me with his fingers. He can hear my breathing getting faster and he slides a third finger into me. I moan and try to stand a little taller.

I'm getting closer and closer. He kisses me harder, muffling my cries as I cum. Leaning back a little, I bring his hand up and suck his fingers into my mouth, licking my cum off them. I look him dead in the eye as I do, making him moan as he feels them hit the back of my throat.

I place both my hands on his chest, with just enough pressure to push him back into the water. I feel it running down his body as I lean in and kiss his chest, working my way down his body. I slide his cock into my mouth and hear him moan, music to my ears! I suck a little harder.

The water washes over my face as I feel him grasp the back of my head with both his hands. I grip his ass, digging my nails in and choke a little with all the water running over my face. Mike changes positions, blocking some of the water and I push his cock further down my throat.

'Fuck, baby, keep that up and I'll shoot my load right down your throat.' His voice sounds so husky and so fucking hot, I suck a little faster, making sure it's hitting the back of my throat, listening to him moaning and feeling his grip on my head tighten. He has me dripping wet. Before he cums I stop and stand up. He bends me over, facing the corner of the shower, water running down my back and ass. As I feel him slide into my ass I moan deep in my throat.

I've been waiting a long time to feel that! He moves slowly at first. I rock back on him, making sure his entire length is in me. Feeling that, Mike grabs my hips and pounds my ass till we are both cumming.

As I stand back up, I feel his arms wrap around me. He rests his head on my shoulder and kisses my neck.

'Get clean, sweetheart, so I can make you dirty again later.'

I laugh, turning my head slightly and he kisses me. There's so much in that kiss. I stumble a little as he releases me from it. He can see the bliss written all over my face. There's nowhere else I want to be. Kissing my forehead he steps out of the shower.

'I'm going to get hot coffee. I'll see you soon, Marie!' And he's gone.

I stand in the shower for a long minute just letting the feelings wash over me. Happy, love, bliss, fulfilled, complete. That one I stick on as I turn the shower off.

Mike completes me, in ways others never have. For now, I push the thought away, more out of protection than anything else. I've been burnt before.

Five minutes later, I'm drinking coffee and rolling a smoke. I look over at Mike and he is smiling at me. I get instant butterflies.

'What?!'

He can see me blush.

'Nothing.'

He continues grinning at me.

'Fuck! What?'

He laughs at me. I mumble under my breath and Mike walks towards me.

'You're cute, I kinda love you... a little bit.' He smiles at me. His hand showing me what a little bit is.

'Love you more, babe.'

$\mathcal{Chapter}$ 12

Mike still had to work as he didn't really have a lot of time to prepare for me to be here. I kissed him goodbye that morning and decided to check the beach out and, to help with my fear of big dogs, I took Susie with me. She's a good dog and is growing on me. Mike only lives two minutes from the beach and once we get there, I let Susie off her leash. She doesn't go far and seems to want to stay relatively close to me.

I find a nice spot on the beach and sit and watch Susie playing in the waves for a while. Once she's tired, she comes back and lays next to me.

I was thinking about the complete feeling I'd had since being here. I'm not sure why but it's becoming the centre of everything I feel. I haven't told Mike how I feel, although I am sure he can see it in everything I do – every touch, every kiss, every time I tell him I love him. I've never felt like this before. I look at Susie and she seems content.

'Ready to go home, puppy?' She lifts her head as if to acknowledge me and I stand up. I don't bother with the leash this time. Susie is worn out and happy just to walk beside me. As we get back, she races up to the house and drinks as much water as she can. I watch her and think, next time take water! Got it. Susie goes and lays out in the sun to dry off.

I walk into the house and decide to call Tash. I miss her and I want to catch her up with everything. I really haven't had a moment to talk to her.

'Hello, you gorgeous lady! How's the sex?'

I choke out a laugh.

'Jesus, Tash, at least give me a minute to get comfy before hitting me with the hard questions!' I make a cup of tea and go sit outside, watching Susie sleep.

I spend a good two hours speaking to Tash, telling her about everything and finally make it to the feeling of completeness that I've been feeling. Tash doesn't even balk at it.

'He's your soul mate, hun. Of course you feel like that!' Tash is right. 'Just give him time to see it too.'

How does she do that?! She sees everything. We talk for a little while longer and then say our goodbyes.

'Before you go, when are you coming to visit?'

Tash goes quiet for a minute.

'I'm not sure yet. But I will let you know within the week. Love you! Go do the things and stuffs! Bye!'

She hangs up before I can ask why. Oh well, it's not like I'm not used to this side of her.

I look over at Susie and I swear to god that dog was listening to me and Tash. She comes over and puts her head in my lap. She looks up at me and whines. I pet her head and watch the horizon; it looks like a storm is building. I close my eyes for what I thought was a second. Next thing I know Mike is kissing my forehead.

'Hello, baby girl.' Mike is smiling down at me. Susie was literally dancing on the spot, she was so excited to see him. I felt the same way! 'Let's go out for dinner tonight,' he said as he pets Susie to calm her down some.

'Oh, that sounds nice! Do I need to get changed?'

'Nah, just the local I think.' Mike pulled me up out of my chair. 'Let's go, I'm hungry.'

Now that he said it, I was starving. 'I don't think I've eaten today. I took Susie down to the beach and then spoke to Tash and passed out apparently.'

'You haven't eaten all day? Is that what I'm hearing?' Mike sounded mildly annoyed.

'Umm, well, I had my coffee this morning and Susie really wanted to go for a walk so it's really her fault when you think about it.' Yep, I threw his dog under the bus!

Mike eyed me and then Susie. The dog clearly knew something I didn't because she picked that moment to leave the porch and hide under his truck. I watched her go and thanked her for her help silently in my head.

I turned my attention back to Mike. He looked annoyed too.

'Let's go babe. I promise I'll eat lunch at the very least from now on.' I reached out for his hand.

'Okay, let's go.' He took my hand, and we went out for dinner.

The local bar was an open air beach side building. One side was almost directly on the beach, with a bar and stools along the counter and the other side was more closed off. It had a dining area and a bar as well. I could see a pool table off to one side.

It's nice being out on a date night. We haven't really spoken too much but we are having fun, good food and drinks. We share a few laughs and then head back to his place. I want to call it home, but it wasn't mine... yet. Mike's hand is resting on my thigh as he drives. I'm staring out the window, there's a full moon and everything is lit up, it's pretty in a cold kind of way. Mike squeezes my thigh.

'What's on your mind, baby? You've been a little quiet tonight.'

I look over at him; my heart couldn't be fuller. I'm with the one person who, even at my absolute worst, found something in me to love.

'It's nothing, babe.' I feel the car slow a little. I cast eyes at the speedo and see he's slowing down and then pulls over.

'Come on,' Mike says to me as he parks the truck.

'Where are we going?'

We are literally in the middle of nowhere. I get out of the car, and he takes my hand, pulling me forward, wrapping his arms around me and guiding me to the cliff face. The view in the moonlight is breathtaking. Everything was blanketed in the cool white light of the full moon, the ocean glistened as it moved below me.

'You needed some head space, you've got it!' He kisses my head, hands me his jacket and goes back to the truck. I hadn't told him I needed head space. The wind is so cold, thank god for the jacket! I sink to the ground, watching the waves and the moonlight moving across them as they crash into the beach.

When I finally came back to him in the truck, he smiles at me. I don't think I've been gone overly long, but when I look at the clock on the dash it's been a good forty-five minutes.

'Jesus, babe, I'm sorry!' I lean over and kiss him. I linger just long enough to savour the feel of his lips on mine and that's all it takes, his hands come up and hold my head in place. Mike kisses me with everything he is. I almost forget how to breathe and when he pulls back and releases my head, I fall forward a little.

'Sorry, baby.' I half laugh, and I can feel the red in my cheeks.

'Falling for me?'

My blush deepens a little bit.

'Bit late for that, babe, I've been yours for longer than I can remember.' I shuffle back in my seat as he starts the truck. We aren't all that far from where he lives so the last part of the trip is over quickly. I follow him inside, my teeth chattering. I'm fucking freezing!

'Cold, honey?'

I nod my head and find the warmest part of the room. It ain't that warm! 'Mike, I'm freezing my ass off!'

He walks over to me and wraps me up. I'm shaking. 'You spent too long on that cliff face and in that wind!'

He's blaming me?! Huh!

'It was pretty, but fucking cold!' I say as he rubs my arms in an effort to warm me up a bit.

'I know how to warm you up, sweetheart,' he whispers in my ear. The jolts that runs through me should be illegal – instantly wet!

'Sharing is caring,' I mumble and feel him lean into me a little bit, then he takes my hand and pulls me after him.

On the way to the bedroom, he starts undressing me, leaving a trail of clothes, a reminder for the morning. By the time we get to the bedroom, we are naked. The door is closed, and he pushes me up against it. It's cold and I gasp as he kisses me. That feeling of his tongue in my mouth has me refocusing on that affection and forgetting the door is cold and I'm shivering. He opens the door and I fall back a little, but he has me in his grasp, stepping forward, still kissing me, guiding me backwards. As we get closer to the bed, he turns us around and pulls me down on top of him. Feeling him under me, the heat coming off his skin, his hands running down my back to my ass – bliss! I kiss his neck, slowly working down to his chest, stomach and hips. I wrap my fingers around his shaft, gently sucking his balls into my mouth, making him moan and I slowly lick up the length of his cock, sucking the head into my mouth. I run my tongue around the head while increasing the pressure and taking more and more into my mouth until I feel it touching the back of my throat.

I feel his hands on my head. I reach up and grab his hands, pinning them to the bed, sucking a little deeper down my throat making him thrust his hips. I can feel his arms straining against my hands, holding them in place. He could easily break my hold if he chose to. Mike continues thrusting into my throat and every time he does, I pull my head back, frustrating him to the point he growls at me. 'Jesus, woman!'

I look up at him and he can see who's playing with him, my kinkier side finally making her appearance. I suck his entire length into my mouth and just as I'm about to pull back again, feeling him ready to thrust, he breaks the hold I have on his wrists and grips my head firmly, preventing me pulling back. He fucks my throat hard. I'm gagging and choking, saliva running down his length. I moan. Mike rolls me over, cock still down my throat, pinning my arms down and sliding his cock down my throat. He knows he's hitting the sweet spot when my body stiffens under him. He starts rocking back and forth, getting faster and faster. He can feel me struggling. He slows down a bit and pulls back enough to let me breathe. I suck in air and try to turn my head, but his knees prevent me from moving. I look up at him and he's grinning at me.

'Don't move.' He repositions himself, cock down my throat, lips locking around my clit.

Ooooh my god, that feels good. He can feel me moaning around his cock. He sucks a little harder, making me lift my head, which forces his cock further down my throat. I choke.

He starts grinding down on my face, apparently liking the way my throat closes around his cock when I choke on it. I'm getting close, my nails are digging into his back and I'm squirming as much as I can with his whole body holding me in place. He stops just shy of my orgasm and can hear me crack up even with his cock all the way down my throat and my mouth full.

'Awww, baby, you wanna cum?'

I growl at him, still not able to talk. He pushes up with his arms, forcing his cock in as far as it will go. He grinds down a little more, knowing full well there's no oxygen getting in and holds it another thirty to forty seconds then slowly pulls his cock out of my throat. I cough and gasp for air.

'Holy fuck!' I manage before Mike rolls me over, pushing my head into the mattress and pulling my ass up into the air. I feel him spit on my ass. Seconds later I gasp as his cock slides into it. He fucks me until we both cum hard. I collapse, him right next to me.

I turn my head and smile. I lean over, kissing his cheek. 'I'm going for a shower, lover. I'll be back soon.'

'I may be asleep when you come back, baby. I'm sorry.'

I kiss his forehead. 'Sleep, honey.'

I walk into the bathroom. So overwhelmed with emotions, everything just seems too perfect. Nothing is ever this perfect. I feel the tears well up and spill over.

Chapter 13

I wake up early, make a coffee and head outside to the patio. I place the mug and my phone with earbuds attached on the small wooden table he has outside. I roll a smoke and sit back in the seat to text Tash, placing the earbuds into my ears and selecting some music and wait for Mike to wake up.

I'm sitting with my knees pulled up, a blanket over me, humming to the music in my ears, cigarette in one hand and my phone in the other. *Who tf cries after sex?!* Tash asks. *Was it that good?*

Fuck yesssss!! I could do that all day long! I nod my head as I answer her text.

Mike casts a shadow and I close my phone instinctively.

I remove an earbud from my ear. 'Morning, honey,' I say without turning around. He kisses the top of my head. I didn't realise he was that close to me.

'Good morning. What time did you get up?'

I stay silent long enough that he nudges me a little. 'Baby girl?'

I turn my head a little and take out the other earbud. 'Early, babe.'

Mike moves around to the other side of me so he can see me properly and knows almost straight away that I didn't sleep much, if at all.

'You look tired, Marie. How early?'

I bite my lip, knowing I'm not going to tell him.

'How's Tash?' The subject change throws me.

'How do you know I was talking to Tash?'

He laughs at me – yeah, I'm always talking to Tash. I must be tired. 'She's good. We were just catching up.'

Mike puts a hand on my knee, the feeling sending a jolt right through my body, making me suck a breath in and I finally look up.

Mike kneels in front of me. 'Kiss me, baby.'

I scoot forward in my chair, bring both my hands to his face and kiss him as I wrap my legs around him to bring him as close as I can. It literally takes my breath away. How the hell does he keep doing that?! I sit back a little but keep my eyes closed and slightly unwrap my legs. My phone buzzes again. Mike picks it up.

'What's the code?'

I laugh at him; he ain't getting that! 'It's a secret and you don't want to read my convos with Tash.'

He smiles at me. 'Oh, I think I do,' he says with a cheeky grin on his face. 'I'll hold on to it for now.' He watches me for a second.

'Don't lock my SIM card trying to figure that out, okay? I'm going to have a shower and wash this tired away.' I stand up, kiss him briefly on the corner of his mouth and walk inside.

There he is with my phone and no way to access it.

As I walk in the door, I see him pick up his own phone and I wonder if he is going to call Tash as I head inside. Tash would tell him if he asked.

Fifteen minutes later I'm standing in the shower, just letting the water run over me, trying hard to wash the tired off and failing miserably, but it feels nice. With water running on my head, I don't hear Mike come into the bathroom. I don't hear him open and close the shower door and only realise he's there when his hands grip my hips. I gasp, partly in shock, partly turned on.

'Hi, baby.' He pulls me closer and plants his lips on my neck.

I moan and bring one of my hands up to grip the back of his head, grabbing a handful of hair, my other hand holding his hand firmly on my left hip.

'Fuck, you're hot!' he says quietly in my ear as he licks my neck.

I press my back into him. The hand that was on my hip shakes my grip and makes its way up to my breast. As soon as his hand touches my breast I moan again. Mike spins me around, pushes me up against the wall of the shower and kisses me, pressing his body in as close as he can, hearing me whimper with desire. He seems to know, even though we can't get much closer, I need more. I slide my hands down his back, slowly making my way to his ass. I feel more than hear him moan when they get there, his tongue in my mouth and his ass in my hands. I'm a hot mess in seconds.

I feel like a wall inside me comes down. I melt into him as he turns the shower off and almost carries me to the bedroom.

'Babe, we're dripping wet!' Mild-ass protest, my voice sounds weak saying it and he ignores me anyway, kissing me again, keeping me in that melted, walls down place.

I can feel the heat coming off his body. I shiver a little and he wraps his arms around me, pushing me closer and closer to the bed. As soon as I hit the bed, he's right there with me, as if he knows that any sudden moves on his part right now could have me closing off and he wants and craves all that emotion is sitting just under the surface...

He's been kissing me for a while. Every time I break away for a second, he licks my bottom lip and has me demanding his lips back. He rolls me on top of him. The sudden change awakens a fever in me. I kiss and bite his neck and make my way down his body, sucking the tip of his cock into my mouth. I grip the shaft with my hand and moan as I lick and suck it. He's got me worked up enough that those walls aren't coming back up as long as I'm focused on his body.

'Baby girl... Sit that pussy on my face.' His voice is so damn husky, I growl a little. I want what I've got right now. 'Don't growl at me.'

I look up at him. As soon as my eyes lock on his, I know I'll do anything he asks. 'Now, baby!' he says, quietly but firmly.

Demanding but not harsh, I push his cock all the way down my throat and stand up, all at once hearing his gasps as he feels his cock hit the back of my throat and leave it just as fast. I do as asked; he has me grinding on his face within seconds. Mike hears me getting close but forces me to stop before I cum, pushing me up.

'Lay down, Marie.'

Hearing my name snaps me back to the here and now. As if sensing that wall snapping back up and needing to stop it, he kisses his way up my body, feeling me squirm under his lips every time they touch my body. Pinning my arms above my head he kisses me again, refusing to leave my lips until he feels that heat again. Holding my hands pinned above my head with one of his hands, he runs his other hand down my body, his fingers leaving trails of fire down my body until he finds my clit. I moan the second he touches it, pushing my pussy into his hand.

I'm getting close again, but he seems to want me exactly where I am. He's waiting out that emotion I've got sitting there just under the surface. He stops rubbing my clit and I snarl at him; he kisses me again. There's a difference in the kiss now, as it contains all the need and want. I'm not melting anymore, I'm closer to catching on fire – he wants that. He teases me a little more, keeping me close but not letting me tip over, his expression showing his enjoyment as he feels me straining against his grip. My whole body is moving to his touches and I'm moaning, snarling and growling at him!

'Let me cum!' I half sob, half snarl.

'Not yet, baby,' he continues teasing me. I manage to get one hand free and have a hand full of his hair in seconds. I kiss him hard, mashing my lips on his. He keeps pushing me, knowing where he wants me.

He teases my nipples at first with his hand and then with his tongue. He has me panting, begging, pleading but he still tells me no. I practically scream at him. I push him off me, pin his shoulders to the bed and slide his cock into me. I grind down hard on him as I sit up. I bring my hands up to my breasts, twisting my nipples a little. Mike watches me, hands on my hips, pulling me down harder.

'Cum for me, baby,' he whispers at me. I snarl again, grinding down harder on his cock.

I cum hard. I don't stop and I know he can see my tears.

Rolling me over, he slows everything down, kissing me.

'Baby girl.' He kisses where the tears are. I can't talk, I'm choked up. I feel his lips brush mine and I kiss him, tears streaming down my face. I've got no control over them.

'Make love to me, Mike,' I whisper on his lips. There's so much emotion in that whisper, he instantly wraps me in his arms and does as I asked – practically pleaded for. Mike holds me close, making love to me. I move with him, almost like we are one. I can tell he is listening to me, hearing the change in my moans, from needing to wanting, from growling to the sweetest sounds… I'm close.

'Tell me when, baby girl.'

I moan louder, gripping his shoulders. 'Oooooh my god, now babe!' I breathe out. We cum together. He kisses my swollen lips.

'Marie?'

I don't open my eyes.

'Mhm?' is all I can manage.

'I love you.'

Tears, god damn it! I curl into his chest and finally sleep. As I'm falling asleep, I whisper, 'I love you, Mike.'

As I drift off to sleep, I feel Mike get up off the bed and hear him walk to the doorway after finding something to wear. I finally fall into a deep sleep as I hear Mike say, 'Keep her company, girl.' He lets Susie into the bedroom and I feel her warmth as she curls up to my back.

Chapter 14

Mike

I walk out to the patio and pick up my phone, looking for Tash's number. Little did Marie know that Tash and I have spoken a few times.

'Hola, Tash, how have you been?'

'Hi, Mike, how's my girl?' Tash sounds tired.

'At the moment, out cold. Susie is keeping her company. Tash, is she okay?'

Tash is quiet for a minute. 'She's... I'm not sure I should tell you, Mike. I'm sorry.'

'I just need to know she's going to be okay? She seems upset – no, not upset... there's something there though.'

'Just love her, Mike. Marie is one of those people that will throw a wall up without a second thought to protect herself if she feels like she's going to get hurt. I've watched her do it before. Once it's there it's damn near impossible to move it. Marie is an amazing person. She loves deeply, but she's been hurt before and will run before she lets it happen again.' Tash takes a breath. 'Mike, you do know that the fact that she flew for you screams how much she loves you? She refused to fly to me when we were a few states apart and she flew over an ocean for you.' Tash laughs softly. 'She loves you that much.'

I'm thoughtful for a minute taking in Tash's words. 'I have no intention of being the reason Marie runs, builds another wall or feels anything but loved and special. She's my person.'

'Marie doesn't do vulnerable – she needs to see that being that vulnerable with you is okay.'

'Thanks, Tash. I'll let you know when she's awake if you wanna call her later. See you soon.'

I hang the phone up and think for a while. I walk into the kitchen and decide to cook something for her. She'll be awake soon and no doubt starving considering the amount of sex and lack of sleep she's had recently. I smile to myself at the thought of her skin under my hands, the memory keeping me company as I prepare lunch for Marie.

***

Marie

I wake up and feel Susie laying behind me. I roll over and pet her. 'Keeping me company, girl?'

She licks my hand. I lay there petting the dog and think about the way I felt while he was making love to me. It was raw and open, like I could be just me, the real me. I know those walls are up again. I also know that letting them down completely makes me vulnerable. I've never been comfortable with vulnerable. Tash has always told me I can be strong and vulnerable at the same time. I just don't know how and I'm not sure it would do more than leave me an easier target to have my heart ripped out and broken. Is that something I think Mike is capable of doing to me? Leaving me crushed and broken... Sometimes. I don't think it would ever be intentional, he isn't like that. In the end we both could really hurt each other. All I want is my life with him. Tash would tell me to just tell him what I want, feel and need. I don't know how to find the words for that, not yet, and I also don't want to scare him away. We have known each other for eight months now. I've been here for two weeks.

Susie gets up and pushes the door open. Within seconds I can smell why she got up. I get out of bed and find something to wear, walking out the bedroom door.

'You better not have woken her up!' I can hear Mike talking to his dog and it makes me smile. I walk silently down the hallway and slowly peek into the kitchen. There's my guy, cooking and feeding Susie the scraps. I lean back on the wall and watch him a while longer.

He seems so happy and content. I can hear him singing softly, talking to his dog and did he just shake his ass? I stifle a laugh. Susie looks over at me and I shake my head at her, like she is going to understand not to give me away! She nudges Mike's leg and I glare at her. He pets her head but ignores the nudge. He's stirring something. Susie nudges him again.

'What is it? What do you want? You can see I'm cooking, and you know you shouldn't be in here!' The way he says it almost makes me laugh out loud. He is so cute when he talks to his dog! Why the fuck doesn't he talk to me like that? I pout.

I slowly sneak past the kitchen and head out onto the porch. I don't want to disturb him and Susie would give me away for sure. I roll a smoke and spy my phone sitting on the arm of a chair. I walk over and pick it up. I scroll through the messages from Tash. Nothing overly interesting.

Hi, babe! Sorry, I passed out finally. I needed the sleep tbh! I haven't slept well for the last week or two.

I sit in the seat and look out over the view, pulling my legs up under me and hugging my knees. I still feel a little off, like it's all slipping away and if I hold on too hard it will all fall apart in my fingers. How do I even go about telling him that? I don't know how to explain to him that I feel like I might wake up and it'll all be gone.

I hear a foot fall behind me and spin around in my chair. 'You should be in bed, baby. You really need to sleep more.' He's right.

Susie comes over to me, sits at my feet and nudges me. 'Huh! She doesn't normally do that to anyone else. She must like you.'

I look up at him, my heart skipping a beat. My god, this man is under my skin. *Ding.* I look at my phone. It's Tash.

'I made you something to eat. Come eat then call Tash if you want?' he asks, doesn't tell or demand.

I stand up and walk toward him. 'Okay, hun.' I stop and stand on my tippy toes, kissing his cheek. 'So, what are we eating?'

He takes my hand and leads me into the kitchen. 'Sit.' He indicates the stool at the counter. I sit as he puts a plate of food in front of me.

'Ahh, that's a lot of food.' I'm quiet but I swear I can hear his eyes roll from the other side of the kitchen. I giggle.

'Eat, babe!' He turns to me and watches as I start to eat. 'Good.'

'Sorry, by the way,' I mumble around my food.

'Nothing to be sorry for. And I'm not sure why you're apologising.' He sounds unsure. Maybe I should just leave it be.

'Never mind then. This is good, by the way.' It is yummy and I am starving. He has made a bacon, egg and onion tartlet, which has a whole lot of herbs and spices I couldn't pick out.

'I spoke to Tash earlier...'

I almost choke on what I'm trying to swallow. He spoke to Tash?! Why hadn't she told me that? Inwardly, I am screaming!

'Oh? How is she?' Outwardly I'm holding it together, I hoped.

'She sounded like she might be missing you a little.'

'What did you talk about?' Oh shit, too direct.

'You.' That stopped me eating right there, a fork full of food hanging in the air. 'Is there something on your mind, baby?'

'I think I'm just tired, I'm not sleeping overly well.' Tash is dead! 'I think I'm going to call her. I'll be back soon. Thank you!' I blow him a kiss, pick up my phone and walk back outside to where I was sitting earlier. Susie is still there. She looks up at me as I come out but doesn't move.

'Hello, gorgeous!' Tash always sounds happy.

'Hey.'

'What's wrong?' There's an instant change in her voice; she knows I've spoken to Mike.

'You spoke to Mike earlier?' I don't know why but I feel betrayed.

'Honey, he loves you and was just worried about you.'

'Why wouldn't he just ask me?' I know the answer to that. I'm not always approachable and I am closed off.

'Do you really want me to answer that?' She knew what she was doing! Ugh!

'Out with it, Tash! I'm listening.' I take a deep breath and wait.

'We need to talk about your walls... Are you ready?'

'They're fine where they are!' I'm instantly defensive. I shake my head at myself. 'Okay, Tash, I promise I'm listening.'

'Buckle up, hun! You need to listen to me... Promise?'

'Promise. I'm listening. I won't say anything until you're done.'

'Okay, good! Being vulnerable isn't a bad thing. Yes, it opens you up to feeling hurt on a level you may have never felt before, but it also lets you get to feel all the wonderful things too, deeply. Even when you're vulnerable, you're strong enough to open up and be that soft, beautiful human with the right people. He is the right people, honey.' Tash finishes talking and I stay quiet a long time. She doesn't say anything else; she lets me process. I'm crying but she waits.

'You know I've always been the strong one, Tash. I can't be hurt like that.' I'm nearly whispering at this point.

'Marie, this is what you wanted and worked towards. Now all you have to do is embrace it. So go embrace it.' She's right. 'Remember I love you and I will see you soon.'

'I love you.' I hang up. I hadn't realised that Susie had come and rested her head on my leg. She's watching me; her eyes look sad. 'I'm okay, girl. Just need to stay out of my head and remember that man in there loves me.' I take a deep breath to steady myself some.

I stand up and turn to head inside and Mike is standing there. I shoot the dog a glare. I swear she knew and didn't tell me!

'Come on, baby girl. Come watch a movie with me.'

Chapter 15

A few weeks roll by, and I seem to have moved past whatever was giving me the feels. Mike and I have been good, great even. He has been trying to teach me about hockey... and failing miserably, but I've stopped falling asleep during the games now. It seems to make him happy, possibly because I'm not snoring through his games any more... but we'll never know because I refuse to ask and he knows better than to say anything.

I can hear him watching a hockey game. I just got home (yes, it feels like home now) from doing the things and stuffs – he hasn't heard me yet. I go get changed because I'm cold and wet after getting caught in a storm. When I walk into the lounge, he doesn't see me straight away.

'Hiya, baby.'

Mike turns and looks at me, smiles. 'Hey.'

He looks straight back to the game. Hmm, I can fix his attention. I walk over and stand in front of him.

'Woman! Not see through!'

I smile at him and kneel down in front of him. 'Better, baby?'

He looks me in the eyes and then down to my half smirking lips. 'Whatcha doing, baby?'

I smile at him again but don't say a word as my hands come up to his jeans. I pop the button, my eyes never leaving his as I undo the fly and bring his cock out.

He adjusts in his seat so I can access that gorgeous cock a little easier. I lean forward, sucking the tip. I feel his hand instinctively rest on my head. I stop.

'Baby, I need you to do something for me.'

'What do you want?' He's distracted between me and the game he was watching.

'Sit on your hands and don't move them till I say.' That got his attention!

'Wait! What?'

'You heard me just fine. I can wait.' I rock back on my knees resting on my heels, drop my hands into my lap and watch him, a smile on my face.

'What are you up to?'

I say nothing, just smirk at him.

'Fuck, woman! You're such a brat!' He sounds genuinely annoyed that he can't touch me.

I laugh. 'When you're ready, honey.' I'm watching him closely. 'There's rules tonight, baby.'

My smile changes a little. It's about then Mike seems to realise I'm going to fuck with his whole game and there's still two and a half periods to go. I laugh, seeing the realisation dawn on him.

'I can go if you want, gorgeous.'

At my words he asks, 'Is that a threat, sweetheart?'

I smile again. My eyes drop to his cock, and I lick my lips then slowly bite my bottom lip.

'God damn it, woman!' He places his hands behind his back. As soon as I see that, I move forward, his cock sliding into my mouth, making him moan. I hear the *whistle*. I stop.

'Baby! What the fuck?'

His cock is still in my mouth but I'm doing nothing with it. I feel him move his hand. I remove his member from my mouth, and I sit back on my heels again.

'No, no, baby.'

I watch him place his hand back. I turn my head and check the game, turning back to him and smiling.

'That was just evil, baby,' Mike says grumpily.

I laugh and lick the tip of his cock. 'My rules, babe. Sit back and enjoy.'

I hear the *whistle* again and suck his cock into my mouth hard.

'God damn, baby!'

I continue sucking his cock, listening to him moan. *Whistle*. I stop.

'Fuck!'

I hear the *whistle* again and suck his cock deep into my throat. *Whistle*. I stop. He thrusts his hips up a little and I take his cock out of my mouth.

'No, no, baby.'

I grin at him. He lets out the cutest frustrated sound, making me laugh. 'I'm just getting started!'

Whistle. I instantly take his cock back into my mouth, making him grunt a little bit. Another *whistle*. I stop again.

'Fucking hell, woman!'

Whistle. I deep throat him; he now knows what the game is. The next *whistle*, I remove his cock completely from my mouth.

'I'll mute the TV.' Mike almost yells it at me.

I giggle. 'That's okay, baby. I can go start dinner instead.'

He shoots me the angriest face I've seen in a while, making me laugh hard. Just as he's about to get yell-y, *whistle* – his cock hits the back of my throat so fast that the moan that escapes his lips makes me instantly wet. I suck a little harder, listening to him enjoying himself.

I'm working him a little harder because I want him close before the next whistle. Hearing him moaning is music to my ears. *Whistle* – I stop again, and I swear to god I hear him whimper a little.

'You okay, honey?' I ask, his frustrated sound happens again and it makes me grin at him.

'I'm going to kick your ass, sweetheart!' he says through gritted teeth as I laugh hard.

'Bring it!'

Whistle. Before he can move, I deep throat him again, making him moan loud, music to my ears. I suck hard. *Whistle*.

'FUCK!'

Whistle. I lick the tip, gently sucking the head. *Whistle*. I hear him groan. *Whistle*. Deep throat. Hearing that change, I feel his hand on my shoulder.

'Honey! Behind your back!' I almost yell it at him.

'Woman, you'd wanna stop playing with me!'

I laugh. 'Make me!'

He goes to move.

'Sit down, I ain't done yet!'

Whistle. I swallow his cock, licking his balls as I do. That moan, oh my god, that sounded so deep. It makes my clit tingle, which has me moaning around his cock! *Whistle.* Yep, that was a whimper for sure! *Whistle.* I make sure he's hitting the back of my throat every time that *whistle* blows. I know he's getting close – I can feel his whole body is stiff and needing a release. I've been driving him mental for a good twenty to thirty minutes now.

Whistle. Knowing it's the end of a period – I've been listening to the game going on behind me the whole time – I stand up.

'Where are you going?' Mike sounds completely incensed and annoyed.

'Nowhere baby, just stretching my legs!' I laugh at him.

He scowls at me and makes to stand up. I can tell by the look on his face that he's ready to just rip my clothes off and fuck me right here on the floor.

'Stay there!' There's steel in my voice and he looks at me, a lazy smile on his face.

'I'm going to play with you later!'

I hear the threat; it sends a jolt through me. I eye him. He's sat back in his seat and there's a smirk on his face. Oh, he wants to play. I decide I'm going to mess with him a little more. I take my shirt and bra off, running my hands up my body grabbing both my breasts and biting my lip all at once, watching him while I do it. I walk back to him and sink down to my knees.

'Ready, baby?'

He chuckles a little. 'Woman, you drive me nuts!'

Whistle. His cock is deep in my throat in seconds, the sound he makes reverberating in my ears. I wanna hear him cum so bad, feel his cock pulsing in my throat. *Whistle.* I stop sucking but leave his cock where it is deep down my throat. He moves a little, moaning at the same time. *Whistle.* I suck down hard, feeling him thrust just a little. He's closer than I thought. *Whistle.* This time, I take his cock out of my mouth.

'FUCKKKK!'

I giggle again. He is so fun to mess with. *Whistle*. I suck him in slowly this time, listening to those amazing moans as his cock just makes the back of my throat.

I start moving a little faster; I'm waiting out the *whistle* but nothing yet. I can feel him stiffening up, although at this point I'm not sure I wanna stop. *Whistle*. I don't stop this time. Within seconds, his hands are gripping my head. He's not letting me up now till he cums. I suck a little harder, moving a little faster. I feel him grab handfuls of hair, just as he shoots his load down my throat. A smile touches the edges of my lips as I slowly raise my head, releasing his throbbing cock.

He laughs a little. 'Jesus, woman!'

I sit back, smile at him. 'Have fun, sexy?'

Mike laughs at me. 'You're so dead!'

I get up and grab my shirt and bra off the floor, keeping an eye on my guy, who I just messed with bad enough that I think he wants to tie me down and have his way with me.

Continuing to keep a safe distance from the riled male in the room, I grab my smokes out of my bag and head towards the door.

'Where are you going?' Oh, that voice. I've heard that voice before. I'm in so much trouble.

'Ahh, I think a smoke is in order... I'll be back,' I say as I put my shirt on while still moving towards the door.

'Just stop right there!' Mike has a little steel in his voice. I eye him from where I'm standing at the door. I see him plant his foot.

'Baby... I'll be right back. I'm taking Susie out.' Hearing her name, she stands up and walks over to me. God love that dog, she is now between me and the slightly annoyed male who missed most of his hockey game.

I push the door open and Susie pushes past me. I'm distracted just long enough that I don't see Mike move. He's on me in seconds. I half squeal and half laugh when I feel his arms wrap around me in a bear hug.

'Jesus, Mike!' I squirm in his grip.

He half carries, half pulls me away from the door, ushering me towards the bedroom.

⤳ Chapter 16 ⤳

Walking into the kitchen the next morning, I see my man making coffee.

'Oooooh, coffee!'

He turns and smiles at me as he hands me a coffee.

'No sugar, right?' I ask absently, still half asleep.

'Did we just meet? I've known you don't have sugar since before you got here,' he says, laughing at me.

Mike stops what he's doing and walks towards me. He takes the mug out of my hand and places it on the counter.

'Hey,' he says.

I look up at him. I know what's coming next and I seriously can't wait to hear those words. 'I love you, girl.' Nothing could wipe the smile off my face right now!

'I love you too, baby.' I pick my coffee up and head outside. I need a smoke and some warmth. I roll my cigarette as Susie comes over for pats and some loving.

I hear Mike come out and watch him as he sits across from me. 'What's on the agenda today, baby?'

It's his day off so I figured we would be doing something together. 'Are you not here today?'

'No, I've got a few things I need to get done. I'll be home after lunch though and then we can do something together if you want?'

I sit, thoughtful for a minute. He normally tells me exactly what he's up to for the day even if he isn't home. I watch him for a second.

'Honey, what are you hiding?' I sound playful but he must hear the underlying tone.

He smiles into his coffee and takes a sip. 'I'm allowed secrets, baby.' He laughs when he sees my eyes narrow.

'What ya up to, baby?'

He eyes me over the rim of his coffee mug.

'Nothing, so stop asking!' Mike shuts down the conversation just like that.

I watch him as I smoke my cigarette. I know he is hiding something, just not sure what. There's a glint in his eyes that makes my stomach do flips.

***

Mike

Heading into the bedroom to get changed, I watch Marie as she does her hair in the bathroom.

'Going out, babe?'

Marie looks over at me and smiles.

'I've got some things to do this morning, but I should be back after lunch.' She laughs after she says it.

Did she just throw my words back at me?

Deciding I'm not playing her game, I walk into the bathroom, spin her around and kiss her.

'Where did that come from?' she asks.

'I just love you!' I walk out of the bathroom, pick up my keys and yell a goodbye as I walk out the door.

Marie has no idea what I have in store for her today. She is going to be blown away. She may well hit me when she sees. But I know it will make her happy and there's nothing I like more than seeing my girl happy.

I continue driving. I should have been there already but, knowing Marie, if I left any earlier, she would have asked more questions.

As I pull up, Tash is there waiting. She waves to me, and I get out of my truck.

'Hi, hun! It's so good to see you!' I hug her tight.

'Hi, Mike! Does she know?'

'Nope, doesn't know a thing and she won't be there when we get back either. So, it's kind of perfect.' Mike smiled wickedly.

'Oh, this will work out great. We will have time when we get back to your place.'

I look at her; she has a devious smile on her face. I'm not sure what I'm taking home with me, but it makes me happy knowing Marie will be happy.

***

Marie

I finish doing my hair and hear Mike yell his goodbye. I just know he's up to something.

'Come on, Susie, let's go!' As soon as she sees me, she starts dancing on the spot. She knows I'm taking her to the little spot we found, a secluded cove away from the rest of the beach. It's tucked away just enough to be private and has palm trees for shade on the really hot days.

I take the leash, but I don't bother putting it on her. She doesn't run too far and always comes back when called or when there's other people around. It's more so I look like I'm doing the right thing.

As we get to the spot, Susie takes off into the ocean. That dog likes to swim! I watch her biting at the waves and start to think. What is that man up to? I saw the look in his eye this morning. He has planned something. But he is being rather sneaky! I might call Tash when I get home and see what she knows.

Susie comes bounding over and gives me the sloppiest kisses and drips all over me. 'Susie! What the hell?' I laugh at her. She licks my face again.

She is just so happy to be out and dances her way back to the ocean with me laughing the whole time. I sit a little while longer, watching her play in the water. We've been gone a good hour or so and I now smell like wet dog, I stand up and start walking. I don't bother calling her; she always catches up to me. I'm going to need a shower now. Thinking of the shower sends a jolt through me. I don't think I've managed to get through many showers without being interrupted in the best possible way by Mike. I smile to myself. I haven't been happier, ever!

As we get to the house, I can see Mike's truck in the drive. Susie runs up to the porch and has a drink as Mike walks out the door.

'Hi, baby!' He sounds suspiciously happy with himself.

'Hi, babe.' I eye him as I walk up the two steps. 'You sound happy,' I say as I kiss his cheek and make to move around him as he throws his arm around my waist.

'Where you going, honey?' he asks as I stop.

'I need a shower. Susie thought I needed to be wet and licked a lot and now I smell like wet dog!' I throw a glare at Susie who just knows I'm talking about her and slinks away to finish drying off.

I attempt to walk past Mike again but he won't let me go.

'Babe! I need a shower!'

He laughs and kisses my forehead. 'You don't smell like wet dog. You smell good though.' His voice drops just a little and the things it does to me should be illegal!

'God damn, babe! You know what that voice does to me!' I swear if he keeps that up, I'll do him right here on the porch!

Mike laughs, a cute as hell, little chuckle that has me instantly wet and stops me pushing on his grasp, preferring to stay right where I am. I'm hoping he does more than just make me edgy. Mike leans in closer as if he senses the change, knowing what that change in me says.

'Maybe later, baby.' He is so close to my ear, his words sending a shiver down my spine. I bite my lip unconsciously. 'And knock that off!' He half growls at me.

'You either need to let me go and have a shower or fix what you started!' I don't look up, my eyes fixed on the front door and my bottom lip planted firmly between my teeth. I feel his grip lessen a little. Okay, he isn't fixing what he started... yet. The rush of instant disappointment is almost overwhelming.

I walk forward as his arm drops. I turn back. 'Baby?'

He looks at me and I can see the heat in his eyes, making me forget what I'm about to say.

'Ummm...' Yep, lost those words.

'Ummm?' he asks, a smile playing on his lips. He knows I'm scrambled.

I laugh a little, feeling instantly nervous. There's something different in that look. I can't quite put my finger on it. 'I... I'm going to... ahhh... have a quick shower.' I manage to get the words out eventually.

'Okay, baby.' Just those two words have me almost stumbling. Not so much the words but the tone he said them in. I grip the door frame as I attempt to walk through it. 'What's up, babbbyyyy?'

I try for a steadying breath. This man has me a hot mess and he has literally done nothing.

I make it through the door and walk as fast as I can to the bathroom, locking the door behind me. Damn that man, how the fuck he does that to me without trying is beyond me! As I'm getting undressed, it dawns on me that there was vodka on the counter. I'm pretty sure it was vodka. I shake my head. I have to be seeing things!

***

Mike

I walk in the front door and look into the lounge.

'She didn't see you, huh?' I laugh.

Tash laughs with him. 'Nope, you had her plenty distracted before she walked in here. Pretty sure she locked the door too!' She laughs harder.

I grab a seat. 'She'll be out soon,' I say as I find a good spot to watch Marie's reaction.

Tash stands up and walks over to a spot behind the door. 'I'm going to make her wet herself! It's the only way!'

I laugh at her as I see the same glint in Tash's eyes that Marie gets right before doing something to cause trouble.

We both hear the bathroom door open and stop talking.

***

Marie

I find something comfortable to wear and head out to find that man that was driving me somewhat crazy. I walk down the hall and stop at the kitchen. Not there, I walk a little further and see him sitting in the lounge.

'Hey, baby.' I walk towards him.

'Hi, honey.' There's something about his smile. Is he hiding something?

'Whatcha doin'?' I stop in the middle of room. I'm uneasy and the look he is giving me isn't helping the matter.

'Me? Sitting here waiting for you.' His eyes shift slightly to just behind my shoulder.

As I go to turn my head, he says, 'Marie, come give me a kiss?'

I stop and look back at him. Yes! Something isn't right!

'What's going on? You've been weird all day!'

He can see I'm ready to lose my shit and he... laughs! LAUGHS?

While I am standing in the middle of the room about ready to get rather yell-y – I mean, he got me all hot and bothered and then is sitting there all cool and calm like he isn't bothered at all! – I feel arms wrap around me. I scream!

'WHAT THE FUCK!'I see Mike lose his shit laughing. The arms get a little tighter. 'MIKE!' He laughs harder and it's about then that I hear the peal of a bell laughter that I've missed so much. 'NATASHA!' I spin around and hug her like there's no tomorrow.

'What are you doing here?' It's muffled but she hears me.

'Mike felt he needed to see us together before he decides you're the one.' She laughed.

'No, no, that's not what I said!' Mike interjects rather quickly. 'Don't throw me under that bus! I've got to sleep next to her!' He laughs.

'Where's the alcohol and what the fuck is with scaring me half to death?' I look at Mike. 'And the secrets?!' I huff. 'You're both dead!' They both laugh louder. As I turn and walk into the kitchen – vodka! I had seen vodka!

Music starts – 'Thot Nation' judging by the beat, Tash's favourite when she's drinking – as I grab the alcohol and glasses. Walking back into the lounge, I see Tash beaming and Mike smiling.

'What are you guys up to?'

Tash turns to me and comes to grab the alcohol.

'Nothing, baby.' Mike looks guilty as sin. But I don't care, Tash is here, and I haven't seen her forever! Mike will keep, I know where he sleeps.

'Roll me a smoke. We have things and stuffs to discuss,' Tash says as she walks out the front door.

'Ooooh! Has he asked yet?' Tash is barely out the door when she asks.

'Asked what, Tash?'

'The questions, of course!' She slaps her forehead.

I laugh. 'No, he hasn't, and I don't know if he ever will… I'm not one hundred per cent sure it matters either.'

'Hmmm, I think it does even if you never actually do it.'

'There's no rush. This is still kinda new even though we knew each other pretty well before I came here. There's plenty of time and no real hurry at this point.'

'If you say so, babe! Let's get fucked up!'

Tash and I get comfy outside and start catching up. I'm sure all Mike can hear is a mass of laughing and giggling. After a while, he comes outs and joins us. All three of us are sitting and laughing and I finally feel like I have my whole family with me. Complete.

Chapter 17

Tash spends the weekend with us and it's amazing. I hadn't realised how much I'd missed her until she was here. It's so much fun just being able to chill and laugh!

'There's my girl!' Mike says as he makes his way over to me. 'How are you?'

I turn and smile at him. 'I'm great, babe. Thank you! It was the best surprise and I've missed seeing her.'

Mike walks closer and pulls me into a hug. 'I love you, girl.'

I melt into his arms and rest my head on his chest and enjoy the closeness and safe feeling it brings me.

'Baby?' I mumble into his chest.

'Yes, honey?'

'I love you.' I squeeze a little tighter. I don't want to let go just yet. I need to feel this for as long as possible.

'Baby girl?'

I look up at him.

'I need to go out for a hot minute, but I'll be back soon. Why don't you curl up and watch a movie? You look tired.'

Tired is an understatement! I find a movie to watch and curl up on the couch. I hadn't really gotten dressed today and am wearing little more than a long t-shirt. I don't think Mike had noticed as leaving the house would have been the last thing on his mind based on his previous reactions to me in that outfit. Although, with Tash here the whole weekend and me being a drunk hot mess all weekend, my poor guy had got little more than a blowjob in the shower... I think, I am almost sure I had done that... could have been a dream. I really don't remember too much of the weekend outside of laughing a lot and having fun with my girl. My mind continues to wander, and I fall asleep.

***

Mike

I walk in and see Marie laying on the couch, sleeping through another movie. Kneeling down next to her, brushing her hair out of her face, she stirs a little. I hold my breath, not wanting to wake her up, just yet... Marie's breathing evens out. It's about then I notice she is pretty much naked from the waist down. It makes me smile as I head to the bedroom.

***

Marie

As I open my eyes I could have sworn Mike was just here. I sit up, stretch and yawn. I hadn't meant to fall asleep; I was just waiting for him to come home. I hear a noise down the hall. Thinking Susie is up to no good, I walk down the hallway and Mike walks out of the bedroom. I jump.

'Fucking Jesus, babe!'

He laughs at me. 'Scare ya, did I? Who did you think was here?'

I lean in and kiss his cheek before turning to walk back to the lounge. Mike places his hands on my hips, stopping me and sending electricity straight through my body.

'Where are you off to?' he asks, pulling me back towards him. I feel his body press up against mine.

'Umm.'

His hands come up to my chest, playfully squeezing my breasts. 'You're staying right here!'

He is determined but playful. I laugh. 'As you wish, baby.'

My feet plant to the spot.

As the bratty note enters my voice, his grip on me tightens a little as he tests out how well I've planted my feet.

'You wanna play, baby girl?'

I turn my head toward his sweet, sexy voice. 'Play?'

He hears the question and smiles.

'Mmm, baby. Let's play!' That damn voice! He has me moving before I remember I was going to stay right there! Fuck!

As I release my stance he uses it to his advantage, pushing me into the bedroom. I stumble a little, but he hasn't actually let go of me, just kept me moving so I can't plant my feet again. Ass!

He's got me stumbling backwards and stops me before I land on the bed.

'On your knees, honey!' he says all husky-like.

Damn! So, demanding and yet so sweet. I sink to my knees. Mike walks away from me.

'What?!'

He turns towards me and... 'Shhh!'

Did he just shhh me?! I glare at him. I go to stand back up and he's on me in a heartbeat.

'I said, on your knees, baby. Stay there!'

I glare at him a little harder.

'Close your eyes.'

Shooting him another glare, I close my eyes while smirking at him.

Mike laughs and I listen to him moving around, although I can't place what he's doing.

I feel him standing in front of me. 'Lift your arms up.'

I do as asked and he takes my shirt off. As I go to put my arms down, he says, 'Leave them up!'

I do as I'm told and feel handcuffs, cold and hard, followed by the sound of a click. I feel tension holding my arms above my head. I open my eyes and peek up. He slaps a blindfold on my eyes.

'I said close your eyes!' There's enough tension pulling me upwards that I'm uncomfortable. I feel his hand on my head. 'Open your mouth, baby.'

I do as demanded, expecting a gag. He slides his cock in.

My lips lock around his shaft. His hands tighten on my head, pulling my hair a little. He moves in a little closer, forcing more of him down my throat, I gag. He pushes in a little further and stops moving.

Just as I choke, he pulls my hands up a little more, making me choke and cry out all at once.

He pushes his hard member in as far as he can, moving slowly at first. Using his hand tangled in my hair he moves my head and starts fucking my throat, listening to me choke and gag. He lets me gasp for air every ten to fifteen thrusts, while I'm drooling all down my chin and chest, tears streaming down my face. I am so turned on, I tingle everywhere.

With his hands pulling my head in, he pulls me in as far as he can. 'Lick them too, babe,' he tells me as his cock is in as far as it can go. When I'm not fighting for air, I can hear him getting closer. He forces his entire length in as far as he can, thrusting long and deep into my throat.

He pulls my hands a little higher, making me cry out around him. My knees only just touching the floor, I try to move, and he thrusts again cumming deep in my throat.

He releases my head and I hear him step back. I suck in air. I'm covered in saliva, which feels cool on my naked body while hanging there.

'That's my girl.' He kisses my cheek.

'Baby, let my hands down?' I whisper in the direction I think he's standing.

'Maybe soon.' I feel his hand on my cheek. 'You look so good like this though baby.'

I hear the vibrator and I whimper. I feel it pulse on my clit and moan loud.

'I want to see you cum first baby, then I might let you down!' He's right next to me. His tongue brushes my ear lobe, lips on my neck, his teeth sinking in slowly making me gasp and moan.

He turns the speed up about halfway on the vibrator. I strain against the cuffs. I moan louder, almost screaming.

'Scream, babe.' His husky voice tipping me over the edge, I scream out an orgasm. He clicks the speed up higher and presses it in a little more.

'Ooooooh my goddd, Mike!' I cry out as another wave hits me.

He turns the vibrator off and kisses me. I've sagged a little, as much as I can with the handcuffs. I'm breathing hard and Mike finally lets my hands down.

'What's for dinner, baby girl?'

I laugh. 'I've already eaten, babe!' I say as I sit up on the bed 'Looks like you're cooking tonight!' I smirk at him and put my shirt back on.

I stand up and he follows me out of the bedroom and into the kitchen. 'Soo, whatcha making me, honey?'

He lifts me up and plants me on the counter.

'Baby, this is not food safe!' I say, laughing. I'm still only wearing a t-shirt, the counter cold on my ass.

'You asked what I'm eating for dinner.' He smiles at me. 'I think I've found it.'

He puts a hand on my chest and pushes me back until I'm laying across the counter. He flicks my swollen clit with his tongue, making me squirm and moan. His lips gently suck my clit into his mouth as he rolls his tongue over it, making me gasp and swear a little.

'Fuck, baby. Oooooh my god, that feels good! Don't stop.' I feel his tongue slide into me, making me grab the back of his head as I grind on his face.

I pull his head in harder and grind a little more, my other hand gripping the counter as I orgasm. Mike grabs my hips and pulls me in closer, continuing to eat me out. I cum again and beg, 'Oh my god, baby, pleassse stop.' But even as I say it, I start grinding again. 'Oh, fuck, baby, don't stop!' I scream out an orgasm, this time sitting up as I cum. He doesn't stop and I grab his head with both hands, pulling his face in hard on my pussy. 'Yesss, babe. Ooooh my god, don't stop.' I feel his tongue enter me again and I lose it. I moan, scream, gasp, pant and squirt.

I collapse on the counter, breathing hard.

Mike stands up and smiles like he has won the lottery. I look at him and laugh. 'Pretty proud of yourself right now, huh?'

He grins at me. 'Who wouldn't be?' He laughs. 'Come on, baby, we need to have a shower and then actually find something to eat!'

I slide off the counter and my legs are jelly. Mike supports me a little as we go have a shower.

After the shower, I fall into bed, ready to pass out. Mike comes out two minutes later to find me curled up in bed, eyes hooded and ready to sleep. He watches me a minute.

'My girl just needed to be fucked silly so she could sleep.' He places a blanket over me and leaves the room. I briefly wake when he comes to bed and wraps me in his arms.

❧ *Chapter 18* ❧

'Morning, baby girl.' Mike brushes past me in the kitchen.

'Hey,' I barely grunt in his direction. I'm in a mood. I can feel it and it will be in his direction if he pokes me today.

'Hey? Not even a good morning?' Mike says it playfully but only gets me glaring at him as a response. 'Not having a good day, baby girl?'

I pick up my coffee and stalk outside. I don't know why I'm moody, but I am in no mood to talk about it just yet. Mike comes out for a smoke but doesn't say anything. For some unknown reason to me, this makes the mood darker. I finish my cigarette and head into the bedroom. I get dressed quickly and walk back outside, leash in hand. As soon as the dog sees it, she's up.

'I'll be back later.'

Mike nods his head but says nothing again. I'm irritated.

I walk down to the spot that I found where no one normally is and plonk my ass down in the sand. Susie, who normally goes straight to the water, doesn't. She lays down about three feet away and watches me.

'What?'

She tips her head to the side and looks at me again.

'Go play.'

She walks down to the water.

I stare off into the distance and try to pinpoint why I'm moody. Everything right up until this morning has been good – no, not good, perfect. Maybe it isn't me and Mike that is the issue…

By the time I realise Susie is lying next to me, she's already dry. How long have I been here? I stand up and walk back to the house. Mike's truck is gone. I walk inside and grab a drink. There's a note on the counter.

I've gone out. Let me know when it's safe to come back. Mike. x

I instantly see red! I walk into the lounge and crank music – as much bass as I can find – and start cleaning stuff so I don't hear the truck roll into the driveway or Mike come into the house a few hours later. I only notice he is there when the music stops. I walk out of the bathroom and into the lounge to find him standing there.

'Any particular reason you turned my shit off?'

'Yep. It's shit. You said it.' Is he poking this on purpose? I watch him for a minute and decide I don't wanna fight.

'Okay.' I walk back to the bedroom, find my earbuds and start my music on my phone, going back to what I was doing. It completely scares me when I turn around and he's standing in the doorway. I ignore him for a few minutes and finish doing what I'm doing.

'I'm going to need you to move out of the doorway,' I say as I take an earbud out.

'I'll move just as soon as you tell me what crawled up your ass this morning.' Mike sounds like he could go either way, yell or listen, depending on my answer. 'Talk to me.'

I take a breath. I've been trying to figure it out most of the day, so how exactly am I meant to tell him what the issue is, if I can't figure it out?

'You were gone for a while this morning. I didn't think you were ever coming back!' He's trying to lighten the mood a little. I don't want to push him away, but I don't know how to let him in either, not just yet.

I look up at him, something I hadn't actually done today. His eyes instantly softens some of my edges. 'I don't know what's wrong,' I say quietly.

'Okay.' He steps out of the way.

I walk forward and just as I get to where he is standing, he reaches out to me. I stop just shy of where his hand is. I really want to be in those arms right now but this mood won't allow it. I can't just yet. I can feel I'm either going to rage or cry at this point. Mike drops his hand – I'm not sure if he can read me well enough to know that it's all there under the surface or if he's admitting defeat. I slip past him and head outside.

I roll a smoke and put the earbud back in, heavy metal floods my ears. I stare off into the distance and feel Susie put her head on my lap. It's enough to break the mood and make me cry. I wipe the tears away and she walks away. Typical! Love me and leave me. I pull the earbuds out. Angry music isn't cutting it anymore. Finishing my cigarette, I stand up and turn around and see the reason the dog moved.

'Baby girl.' His voice is soft. If I just let him, he'd fix it.

I drop my head. I don't want to feel like this anymore. I can't move. I feel the tears and turn back around. I just need to wear myself out so I can sleep and wake up happier. There's no real reason to feel like this. I feel defeated and tired, like I've lost something, but everything is just the same as it was yesterday. A small sob escapes me. Susie stands up and stops.

I feel him standing behind me, but he hasn't touched me yet. 'Honey? Why are you crying?'

There is absolutely no way to tell him anything right now without completely losing it and becoming a crying mess. I feel his hand on my shoulder; my body heaves as I hold in what's trying to get out. He pulls me back a little but doesn't wrap his arms around me. Why can't he just do that?

'Marie, I've come this far. You need to do the rest.' His voice is calm, quiet and sweet.

'I can't,' I whisper. I don't even think he heard me.

'Yes, you can. I'm right here, baby. Always will be,' he whispers in my ear. His voice breaks that something holding me back.

I turn and his arms are around me in an instant. I break and let all the emotion flood out. He weathers it like it's a light breeze. He lets my emotions batter him like its nothing, never letting me go the whole time. There are days I don't think Mike is aware of the effect he's had on my life since coming into it. The day he came into my world was the day I dared to open up and let my heart risk being hurt just to have that little bit of happy he brings to my life.

'I will always be here, honey. You can't get rid of me that easily.'

I cry a little harder at hearing his words. There is literally no way for me to answer him, so I squeeze harder, hoping he won't let me go.

It's about then that it dawns on me that I would have none of this without the app I downloaded almost a year and a half ago now. I wouldn't know what it feels like to be loved like this, laugh like this, be this happy and how easily it could all be gone. I don't think Mike really ever appreciated what I meant when I told him that I would blow up my world to have a chance at this. He is worth all that and so much more. If only I could find the words to tell him all that. But instead, I cry a little more and my man holds me while I do it.

Eventually, I'm all cried out. Mike doesn't ask questions. He just takes me to bed and hugs me tight all night long.

I wake up early and it's still dark. I sit up and Mike is sleeping facing me. I run my finger down the side of his face, watching him sleep and feeling the overwhelming feelings that are still raw and on the surface. I kiss his cheek and slip out of the bed. I absently make a coffee and look for my phone. I need Tash.

I call her. It's super early and I almost hang up just as she answers. 'Hi, gorgeous, is everything okay?'

As soon as I hear her voice the tears spill over but I answer her. 'I feel like I'm going to lose this, Tash.'

'Why do you think that?' She knows me; she knows I'm prone to overthinking, self-sabotaging and feeling like I don't deserve whatever little happiness I find.

'I don't know.' I go quiet.

Tash lets me have my quiet for a few minutes. 'He isn't going anywhere, hun. He was yours before you got there – there is absolutely nothing you could possibly do that would make him run away from you.' She waits a minute before she continues, possibly waiting for me to disagree with her. 'Sweets, when I was there, I saw how he looks at you. He sees nothing but you, only you, always you. You need to trust that. And remember we both love you.'

For a while there is only the sound of me breathing as I take in Tash's words. 'I don't even know why I feel like this, Natasha.'

'Because he is the one, babe! He is the other half that completes your world and makes you whole – embrace it and let him love you the way he wants to, needs to.'

'I love you, Tash.' I hang up, knowing she understands I need to process.

I put my phone down on the coffee table, pick up the dog's leash and head down to town. I need to clear my head. Mike doesn't need another day of this. And I feel like being around people doing normal daily things. People watching was always something I liked to do while drinking coffee back home. Susie is happy sitting under the table eating scraps I gave her.

***

Mike

I wake up and the sun is just peeking over the horizon. I head into the kitchen to get coffee, thinking Marie is outside already. As I get outside, I can see her phone sitting on the coffee table. Thankfully, Marie had told me the code after a few weeks of being here. I open the phone and see a message from Tash. It was sent two hours ago.

Don't overthink it, hun, just embrace it. I love you, lady!!

Checking the call log, I see they had spoken almost three hours ago.

'Susie!' I call my dog and she doesn't come. I instantly know where she is. I'm torn – do I wait for her to come back, or do I go and get her? I know Marie has been a mess the last twenty-four hours, I just don't know why. She never did open up and tell me, she'd just cried herself to sleep in my arms. I'd stayed awake for hours, after she was sleeping soundly, thinking about what could have changed in her world for her to come down that hard.

I sit down and open the phone again.

'Hi, hun, are you okay? You didn't answer me.'

'Hi, Tash, she's not here. But I know where she is.'

'Mike! Where is she?'

'She stole my dog so a good guess is down at the beach.'

Tash laughs. Marie with a dog is just funny. 'Go get our girl, will you!'

I breathe out, like I've been holding my breath waiting to hear those words. 'I'm going, Tash.'

I hang up the phone and grab my shoes. Just as I walk out the door, I see Susie. Looking further down the drive I note there is no Marie. I walk down the drive and find her sitting on a rock at the end of the drive.

***

Marie

I make it to the end of the driveway. I don't think I can walk up to the house. He'd be awake for sure. I should have stayed there. Now, I'm all nervous and can't turn my head off. Seriously, I'm my own worst enemy some days.

'Hi, baby girl. Time to come home.'

I jump at hearing his voice. He came looking for me.

'Take me home, babe.' I reach out for him with my hand. He takes it and I let him walk me up the driveway.

'Are you okay?' Mike asks me.

'No, but I will be.'

We walk in the front door, and he stops me by pulling on my hand. I turn towards him, and he kisses me. Long, deep, perfect. It was exactly what I needed to lock those doubts away.

Chapter 19

Mike

Marie seems to have let whatever she was holding on to go and, with Tash here now, Marie seems content. Although she never did really say what it was that got her to that breaking point and always seems to deflect when asked. I've stopped asking... for now. Marie being happy is all I ever really want.

I've just arrived home and am walking inside when I notice how quiet it is. The girls must be sleeping off another hangover, I think. Making my way to the kitchen I see a note on the counter.

Hi, babbbbyyyyyy!!! We have gone to the bar! Meet us there? I love you long time xxxxxxx

Well, at least I know where they are! After jumping in the shower to wash my day off, I get dressed and head down to the bar to meet the girls.

I walk in and scan the bar. I know they're here just by the music playing. Unmistakable. I see Tash first. Shaking my head, I walk towards her as she's attempting to get up on a table to dance. She sees me and yells, 'MIKE! You gorgeous hunk of man! Come help me up here!'

I do as asked because there's no point telling Tash to stay off a table!

'Where's Marie?' I ask as Tash steadies herself on the table using my shoulder. Tash points in the general direction of the bar.

'She's over there. Some guy was sweet on her!' Realising what she said, Tash clamps her mouth shut. I'm sure my own expression is far from amused. I stalk off to the bar, hearing Tash follow along behind.

***

Marie

'Come on, honey, you know you want some of this!'

I laugh at him, as I move closer to the table and try to take my shot. Just as I go to shoot the ball, Mr Thinks He Can puts his hands on my hips and pulls me back.

'You need to let me go,' I say quietly but the threat isn't missed. I move and go to take my shot again.

'Come on! You know I've got what you need.'

This time one of his friends comes and takes him away. 'Sorry about that. He's had a few too many.'

I nod my head but don't bother saying anything.

'My name's Matt, by the way.'

'Hi, Matt.' I step back from the table as the person I'm playing takes their shot.

Matt walks closer to me, not too close that he's in my space but close enough that I step back instinctively. There's a wall behind me. Fuck!

'What can I do for you, Matt?' I step a little to the side, giving myself a little distance even if it's not much.

'Let me buy you a drink to apologise for my friend's behaviour?' he offers.

I step up to take my turn. Just as I'm about to shoot the ball, Matt steps in behind me and leans over me. I can feel him pressing into me.

'I asked to buy you a drink, the polite thing to do is say yes!' he whispers loudly in my ear.

I look around for Tash. I can hear her but can't see her. I could have sworn she said Mike's name.

'Let me take this shot and you can buy me a drink,' I say nicely enough but inside I'm raging. This asshole is just like his mate, and I've about had enough!

He steps back and, as I take my shot, he grabs my ass. Yep, that's Tash's voice yelling. I turn around just as Mike uppercuts Matt. Down goes Matt.

'We are going home. Now!' The look on his face is enough for me to drop the cue on the table and move. Tash follows me. 'Get in the truck.'

I haven't said a word, but god, I can feel the tension. Tash is quiet too, something she's not always good at. The trip home is quick and when we get there, Tash kisses my cheek, says goodnight and throws a hug on Mike in an effort to soften him some, I'm guessing.

'Goodnight, Tash.' Mike sounds like he is chewing glass. Tash throws her eyes at me, like *hate to be you right now*, and disappears fast.

I haven't looked up at Mike since he knocked Matt out. 'What were you doing?!' He spits the words at me.

I look intently at the floor. 'How's your hand? I'll get you some ice.' As soon as I move, he's on me. His hand is on my throat and my back is against the wall. I'm instantly wet.

'I didn't ask for ice!' He growls at me. 'I asked what you were doing!' He's almost yelling. I don't know why but in this moment, I am so turned on.

I try to talk and can't. Feeling me trying to speak and not being able to, Mike steps back, releasing me.

'I was playing pool. Admittedly, not very well, mainly because of the amount of alcohol, but playing pool.' My words are quiet, more so to prevent a fight over something that was out of my control.

Mike stands there, the tension in his body hasn't lessened at all. I'm unsure if I should move, let alone breathe at this point. I glance up and can see the anger on his face. I shift my feet slightly, drawing his attention straight away, but he doesn't move.

'How's your hand, babe?' I ask but don't move.

'Just don't move.' He growls at me.

'Baby… you need ice.' I step forward half a step. Mistake!

As soon as I move, he's on me again. He pushes me back to the wall, looks me dead in the eyes and says, 'I said don't fucking move!'

I take a breath.

'Baby…' It's all I get out. His lips lock on mine, kissing me hard. Mike presses me harder into the wall. I moan.

He breaks away and says hoarsely, 'Don't fucking move, Marie!' He steps back and turns slightly away from me. I'm confused, I haven't actually done anything wrong.

I stand there, catching my breath. There's something different about Mike. But I'm not sure I want to poke it and find out just how different. I inch half a step to the side. He doesn't notice. I do it again. His hand hits the wall. I stop looking at the floor. His hand is still there, preventing me from moving closer to the kitchen. I am torn between pushing him and staying where I am.

I push. I wouldn't be me if I didn't. I kiss his arm, slowly making my way up past the elbow. As soon as I make it past his elbow, his arm wraps around my neck. I feel it everywhere!

'Why can't you listen?' Mike sounds somewhat choked up as he whispers his words into my ear.

'Baby, I listen, I'm just concerned about your hand.' It's all I get out when he pushes me into the wall again.

'Marie! FUCK!' He actually yells it at me. It's so hard to explain what that sound does to me. It makes me weak at the knees, it makes me so wet, it makes my heart skip a beat, it makes me melt and want to tell him I am his and only his.

'I'm staying right here, Mike, I promise. I'm all yours, baby.' My voice is quiet.

Mike presses up against me, his other hand snaking up my hair and pulling my head back so I'm looking at him. 'I'm going to show you what you mean to me!'

He pulls my head back hard and kisses me violently, biting my lip and making me cry out, pain and pleasure all at once.

'Move!' He pushes me towards the front door.

'Baby?' I stammer.

'I said move!' He grabs my hand and pulls me with him. We make our way to his workshop. He pulls me over to his work bench. 'Take your clothes off now!'

I do as I'm told, as if I have any choice. My clothes come off so fast. I'm standing there naked, and he looks me up and down. I feel exposed, but I'm comfortable with Mike. This is my guy, he loves me.

'Bend over the bench!'

Complying, I bend over the bench. I feel his hand on my back, working down to my ass. *Slap, slap, slap.* On the last one, I cry out. I gasp as I feel my ankles chained down, legs locked apart as far as he can get them. He moves around the bench to my head. I feel him grab my right wrist, stretching it as far as it can go and doing the same with the left, locking them in place.

'Open your mouth.'

I do as asked and he places a gag in my mouth, making sure its tight. He leans down to my ear. 'I'm going to make you scream, baby girl!'

I moan around the gag as he places a blindfold over my eyes. I can feel the wetness dripping down my leg and the anticipation building in me.

I listen intently to him moving around the area. I still don't know what he's doing.

When I feel something bite into my skin, I cry out. It doesn't stop. I try to cry out more and I can't. I feel it bite into me another seven times. I try to scream but have no luck. Mike is back at my head. He removes the gag and replaces it with his cock. He pulls my head up as far as it will go and fucks my throat. I'm gagging, my throat constricting around his cock and just as I can't breathe, he hits me again with the crop. He's moaning at me as I'm trying to scream around his cock. He pulls his cock out of my throat, replacing the gag. He hits me a few more times across my ass before I feel his tongue lick from my clit to ass.

I moan as loud as I can. I can feel an orgasm building. If I could grind back on his face, I would be cumming already, I'm so worked up. He has me locked in hard. He continues to drive me crazy, licking my ass just enough to keep me at that point of orgasm without letting me get there. I try without success to back up on his mouth with no release. I can't move. I drop my head and feel the wetness there, knowing I'm drooling around the gag in my mouth. I try to beg to let him let me cum.

'Did you say something, baby girl?' he says as he flicks my ass again with his tongue. I cry out as much as I can. Just when I think he can't tease me anymore, I hear the vibrator start.

As soon as it hits my clit, I jolt forward, only to feel the work bench bite into my thighs. I attempt to cry out and he turns the speed up one level. I moan louder. I can feel the orgasm is right there. He turns it off. I sob.

'Not yet honey,' he says as I try to take a shuddering breath.

I'm so wet and I can feel it running down my leg. I try to plead, the words lost because of the gag. He releases the feet restraints and I feel my arms lift and he spins me so I'm facing forward. I can feel the bench biting into my lower back. He drops my arms back down on the bench and locks them in. I feel his fingers slide into my pussy. It makes me gasp and bite down on the gag. I want all of him in me, but I know that won't happen yet, if at all. He intends on keeping me at this point of wanting and needing to cum without release.

'You're all mine, always!' There's appreciation in his voice.

I hear the vibrator again, a low hum. Not high enough to let me cum, just enough to drive me insane. I whimper as it touches my clit. At the same time, I feel his fingers grip and twist my nipple. I groan and he twists a little harder. I try to rock on the vibrator. All I'm focused on is the pleasure I can feel radiating from there. Mike chuckles and clicks the vibrator up as high as it goes for three seconds, making me cry out as loud as I can before he switches it off. I could cry! I was right there; I'm still right fucking there! Denied again.

He has me tittering on the edge and, if I could, I would beg him for it! I feel his hands grasp my hips as he plunges his rock-hard cock into me. I whimper and I silently pray he doesn't stop. Feeling him moving in me is ecstasy! My hand is in fists and my moans escalate. As I cum, he places the vibrator on my clit. He turns it up, intensifying my orgasm. Mike continues fucking me, turning the vibrator up again. I scream as I cum.

He has me so focused on cumming just for him that I am blind to everything else around me. I cum again and he turns the vibrator up another notch, watching me strain against the bonds holding me in place. I bite down hard on the gag as another wave washes over me and he turns it up higher, making me shake as ripples of orgasms hit me. My whole world in that moment is focused on the pleasure radiating from my pussy as the pulsing has more orgasms rushing through me. He watches me try to get away from the vibrator, and I cry out when the work bench bites into my back, forcing me to thrust my clit back onto the vibrator and making me cum seemingly endlessly. My chest is heaving as I try to catch my breath, screaming as I cum for this man of mine continuously.

'Jesus baby girl, you're amazing!' I hear him talking but am unable to focus on what is said as another orgasm wracks through my body. I sob a little and he turns the vibrator up to its highest level.

My whole body is taut. I yell as I cum. He thrusts harder into me, grinding forcefully with each orgasm I have. I am cumming constantly but I can feel a build of something larger. My moans change from high pitched to deep and I am almost snarling at Mike.

'Cum again, baby.' His voice is soft; he's ready for what's coming. He has spent this whole time getting me to this point. My legs lock around his waist, pulling him into me more. I cum, growling, my juices flowing out of me and all over Mike as he puts the vibrator down. He pulls out of me and cums on my breasts, belly and watches it run down to my pussy.

I lay there panting, tremors wreaking havoc on my body like aftershocks from an earthquake. Mike reaches up, removes the gag and releases my hands. I work my jaw a little.

'Oh my god, Mike!' I can scarcely whisper at him. He leans down and kisses me, soft and sweet. He lifts me forward and into his arms, holding onto me. I have nothing left. He takes me inside and I fall into bed, asleep as my head hits the pillow.

***

Mike

I watch her sleeping. Reaching over and brushing the hair off her face, I smile. She was just what I needed in my life, and she is all mine. Walking outside and lighting a cigarette, I'm thoughtful. There has been something on my mind for a while now but I just wasn't sure it's what I wanted.

I look up at the stars. Of all the people in all the world, I found her. I know I love her, want her, need her, can see a future with her, but for how long? Does she want forever or just for now? Am I willing to sacrifice for her?

I shake my head and put my cigarette out in the ashtray. I walk back to the bedroom and curl up around my girl. She murmurs and snuggles in.

∽ *Chapter 20* ∽

I wake up late. I can feel every muscle in my body and the feeling brings a smile to my face.

I can hear music playing, so Tash and Mike are already having coffee and, because it is country music, I know they are just chilling. I move slowly, kind of testing out my muscles and how sore they are. I sit on the edge of the bed. I need a shower. I stand up and walk into the bathroom. I start the shower and when the water is the right temperature, I step in. Just feeling the warmth falling all over me is delightful. I stand there, enjoying the easing it brings to my muscles. After my longer-than-normal shower, I head out to the kitchen. I need coffee.

I can hear Tash and Mike talking outside. I grab my coffee and head outside. As soon as they see me, they go quiet.

'Good morning, honey,' Mike says as I come to sit with them.

'Morning!' Tash is way too happy for the way I feel right now.

'Morning. What were you talking about?' I pick up my tobacco to roll a smoke, deliberately not making eye contact with either of them. I have the feeling I interrupted something and really don't feel like being right just yet.

Tash answers first. 'We were discussing when I am going back. Mike apparently is sick of sharing.' She shoots a glare in his direction, making him laugh.

'Uh-uh, I totally believe you, Tash.' She knows I heard something but doesn't know what or how much. 'I might take Susie down the beach soon,' I say into the silence.

'You need to eat first, babe. You had a big night and you both drank a lot. I'll cook you something.' Mike makes to stand up. Is he running away from me?

'You know I never eat anything for breakfast, baby.' I say it without emotion. I feel wiped out; maybe I should eat something.

Tash looks at me then and I'm sure I still look tired. I light my cigarette and look out over the view. I can see the ocean; it's so blue today. I take another drag and zone out, watching the white peaks of the waves break. Mike walks inside, knowing I'll stay where I am till the coffee is gone, giving him at least thirty minutes to get something cooked and making sure I eat before I pass out or waste away.

Tash moves closer to me. 'Sweets, are you okay?' She sounds a little concerned and I look at her so she can see I'm telling her the truth.

'I've never been better, Tash. I'm just tired, it was a... long night.' I trail off and return my stare to the waves crashing onto the beach. Tash leans her head on my shoulder and kisses my cheek while I am reliving the night before in my head. Being completely at Mike's disposal had been a massive turn on for me. I absently chew my nail, remembering how I felt.

I am completely lost in my thoughts when Mike comes back outside with breakfast.

'Baby girl?' He nudges me gently and I refocus on what's in his hand. Food! Okay, so I am hungry. I sit up a little in my chair and realise Tash has disappeared.

'Where's Tash?' I ask as I eye the bacon and eggs that he brought out to me.

'She went back to bed. She ate earlier.'

Earlier – he caught my attention.

'How early were you two up?'

Mike eyes me.

'Eat, baby girl. She was awake at seven o'clock and I was already up. I fed her then. She needed food, just like you do! Eat!' He half laughs and half growls at me. I start eating.

'What were you talking about when I came out, gorgeous?' I don't look up, more to give him time to think of something and to prevent him lying to me.

'We were talking about you. But that's all I'm telling you. Now eat and take Susie out for a while. I know you need your own space, honey.' When did he figure me out so much?

I finish eating and grab my shoes and Susie's leash. I start walking and Susie is up and on my hip within seconds.

I don't bother going to the spot today and sink into the sand as soon as I hit the beach, watching the waves. Susie takes off; she loves the beach.

***

Mike

'Is she gone?' Tash walks out and looks at me.

'Yeah, she didn't even say goodbye!' I know I sound annoyed.

Tash laughs at him. 'You fucked the life out of her last night! I'm surprised she's even awake at this point!' She drops into the wicker chair beside me.

I laugh with her, looking down the driveway to make sure Marie is gone. 'Okay, let's go. Marie is normally gone a few hours when she goes down the beach. We just need to be back before her.'

I grab the keys and Tash gets in the truck.

'Do you think she knows?' Tash asks thoughtfully as we drive to the store.

'She knows something, but she doesn't know this… and I kind of need to keep it that way for now.'

'Marie is smart. She will figure this out quick. Probably a good thing she's tired today.' Tash chuckles. She knows Marie well and if she'd been on her game this morning, there would have been no hiding anything from her. She would have poked at us both till they cracked. Marie has a way of picking up subtleties and following it without error until she has her answers.

'I just need her out of the know for three more days. Then she can know everything.'

'Hun, this is why I'm still here. I'll keep her distracted while you sort this out.' Tash reassures me.

I pull over next to the store as Tash jumps out excitedly. We walk into the store and the salesperson nods to me, bringing out a package I'd ordered.

'So, what do you think?' the salesperson asks.

Tash is speechless.

'She'll love it!' she exclaims.

***

Marie

Susie finally comes back, and I am getting hot, so I head home. As I get into the drive, I notice that Mike's truck has moved. I walked past it when I left and now it's parked down at his workshop. I chew my lip and think.

I have been tired today, but being down near the water has helped clear my head. I see Tash sitting on the porch with my guy. They look happy with themselves.

'Hi, baby!' Mike sounds so happy.

'Hi… what are you two up to?'

I swear I see Tash's mouth form a curse word.

'Mike is about to pour us a drink!' Tash says.

I eye her; something isn't right here. 'I'm not drinking today. I need something cold though, if you don't mind, baby?' I look to Mike who seems more than happy to disappear.

'I'll be right back, sexy.' As he walks past, he kisses my forehead but won't look me in the eyes.

'Right! Tash, out with it!' I glare at her. This woman can't hide things from me.

'Don't poke, Marie. Just leave it alone. Please.' There's something in the way she says that that gives me butterflies. I sit down hard in the seat next to her and refuse to acknowledge the thought that bounces into my head.

'Here you go, baby.' Mike hands me a drink. I take a sip and remember I said I wasn't going to drink. I take Tash's drink and down the whole thing. I cough a little, stand up and walk inside.

Tash follows and watches me pour a shot. 'Marie, are you okay?' I down the shot and hold a finger up to her, cutting her off. I pour another three shots, one after the other, and when I feel the buzz kick in, I do another one.

'I'm great!' I finally answer her. Tash would know I'm about to be hit by a bus; she just watched me down five shots on a basically empty stomach.

I walk back outside and plant a kiss on Mike's lips. 'Baby, we need music!' I say as I stand back up, dizzy instantly. Mike steadies me as he stands up.

'What did she do?' He glances at Tash and Tash makes a shot motion and holds up five fingers while smiling at him. 'Why didn't you stop her?' He sounds slightly annoyed and amused all at once.

Tash shrugs. 'You wanted her distracted, she's distracted!' Tash laughs.

'MUSIC!' I demand from the rail holding me up.

'I'm on it, baby!' Mike walks inside and puts some music on. As he walks back outside, he seems to see the bottle in my hand. 'Baby? Are you going to share that?'

I turn and look at him, grabbing the rail again as Mike steps forward and takes the bottle out of my hand. 'Hey! That's mine!'

'I know, and you can have it back when you're sitting down.'

I glare at him a little. 'Tash! Come dance with me!'

Tash comes over to me, grabs my hands and we start dancing. Tash and I have known each other so long that nothing is off the table, so neither of us are surprised that we are grinding on each other within minutes. From the few glances I shoot in Mike's direction, he doesn't seem to mind either. He seems happy watching his girl grinding on another chick, even if it is Natasha.

'I'll be right back!' Tash disappears and I turn to Mike.

'Come dance with me, baby?' I smile at him, and he seems to blush a little.

'I can't dance like that, baby girl!' He laughs at me.

I smile at him, walking over and straddling him in his chair. I lean in and kiss him, pressing as much as my body into his as I do it. He makes a sound deep in his throat, making me tingle way down deep. I can hear Tash on her way back so I get off Mike and make my way back to where we were dancing a few moments ago. It's about then that Mike seems to realise I took the bottle of tequila with me.

'Jesus, woman! I'm going to be pouring you into bed at this point!'
He walks over to me and takes the bottle back. I protest and Tash
laughs hard. The bottle was almost full when I started doing shots.
There was less than a quarter left. This is going to hurt in the morning!

'I think it's time for my music!' I turn and walk inside. Mike rolls
his eyes, knowing the music is about to get a whole lot louder with
what myself and Tash call 'Thot Nation'.

'I'm too sober for this!' Mike takes a swig out of the bottle, laughing
at me and Tash grinding up on each other.

The night continues. We all get drunker and laugh a lot, dancing,
singing and just having a good time.

At two a.m., Mike takes my hand. He must have noticed I'd been
sitting and trying not to pass out for at least the last thirty minutes.
'Time for bed, girls.'

Tash follows me and disappears into her room. I follow Mike to our
room and fall into bed.

The next morning, I wake up to a glass of water and painkillers
on the bedside table. God love that man! I take the painkiller and roll
over, closing my eyes and hoping the world opens up and swallows
me whole! I feel terrible and have no idea why Tash would let me near
tequila! I will thank her for that when I can move.

Oh, the whole idea of moving makes me feel sick. I stay as still
as possible. I don't remember when I fell back to sleep – somewhere
between cursing Tash out and trying to stop my stomach from rolling
– but when I wake back up, I feel halfway normal. I slip out of bed and
walk straight outside. I need fresh air.

'There she is! Good morning, sweetheart.' Mike kisses my forehead.
'Did you get the painkillers?'

I nod my head in response and instantly regret it. I bring both my
hands up to my pounding head and hold it like I can stop it pounding.
I groan. 'Kill me!' I plead in Mike's direction.

'No, no, I kind of love you a little bit. Want coffee?'

I nod again and glare at him as he laughs at me making the same
mistake again.

'It's not funny, babe! I feel like I've been run over by a train,' I say
harshly but oh so quietly. 'Where's Tash? I'm going to kill her!'

'She was up earlier, and coffee didn't agree with her, so she went back to bed. Who knew you both shouldn't drink tequila.' Mike chuckles as he walks inside to get me a coffee.

It's so bright. I need sunglasses or someone needs to turn the sun off. I can smell the coffee and the smell makes my stomach churn slightly. Not a good sign at all. Mike comes back with the coffee, handing me the mug and then places a glass of water next to me too. I drink the water first.

'Tash said she might be leaving tomorrow.' Mike watches me for a reaction.

I look up and instantly regret it. 'Sunglasses, please,' I plead. He hands me his that he had on his head. 'When did she say that?' I ask, putting the sunglasses on.

'She mentioned it when she was up earlier. She got woken up by a phone call and said she was needed back home.' Mike shrugs.

Tash being needed back home is never a good thing. It's either work or family and Tash, even though she loves her family, doesn't always like dealing with their BS. So, I hope it's work.

I sip my coffee and wait to see if it's going to make me sick or not. When I know it's safe, I drink a little more.

'Hi, guys. I'm going to head off tonight. There are things I need to sort out and it's easier to do back home.' Tash walks towards me and I stand up to give her a hug.

'Everything okay?' I ask and she squeezes me a little tighter.

'It will be. I love you!' Tash whispers in my ear.

She turns and hugs Mike, whispering something to him as well. Something that makes him smile and then try to hide it when it catches my eye. Hungover or not, I haven't seen him smile like that ever – something about it gives me butterflies.

'I called a taxi,' Tash says as it rolls up the drive. 'Remember to call me, like, every day!' She waves and dumps her stuff in the taxi and leaves.

I turn to Mike after the taxi leaves. 'What did she say that made you smile like that?'

Mike giggles, yes, giggles! He never giggles! 'Nothing you need to worry about, baby girl.' He walks forward and kisses my head. 'I'm going to draw you a bath. I think my girl needs to relax a little.'

I watch him walk inside and try to remember where I left my phone. I find it on the kitchen counter.

What did you say to Mike??

Nothing! Now go be with your man and I'll call you when I'm home xxx

I glare at my phone and that thought pops into my head again. It knocks the wind out of me.

'Come on, baby, it's ready.'

I let Mike take me to the bathroom.

Chapter 21

Two days later I still haven't heard from Tash. She's been ignoring my texts and calls. It's so unlike her. She has me worried. I walk into the kitchen, find my earbuds and put music on. I need a distraction – the two most important people in my life are either MIA or acting weird and I just can't deal with it anymore. Speaking of weird, since Tash left, Mike has been acting different. I can't get hold of her to find out what she knows, and he is avoiding questions like they are going to bite him. Remembering the conversation we had this morning, I huff, irritated. I hate being irritated.

'It's a harmless question!' I protest.

Laughing, he kisses me. 'It's far from harmless. I'm going to work; I'll see you tonight.'

UGH! I hadn't even asked anything bad. Just what Tash had said to make *MY GUY* smile like that!

'We're going out tonight so be ready, babe. Goodbye.' He waves and leaves.

I go about cleaning things that don't even need cleaning, but I need to stay busy to prevent myself from thinking things that are just absurd. They both know I'm prone to overthinking EVERYTHING given enough time in my own head. I wipe the same counter over for the fifth time and throw the cloth into the sink. I stomp outside. I know I stomp because Susie, who is happy to see me normally, turns tail and disappears out the back.

Well, that's just great! Now I'm scaring the dog away too. I flop down into one of the chairs and watch a storm building in the horizon. The last time I watched a storm, I ended up here.

The last year or so has been amazing. It was the best decision I have ever made, following my heart, and thankfully Mike hasn't broken it. So why am I so worried about what Tash had said?

It dawns on me that she made him smile the way he used to when he'd wake up and realise I was there and all his before making love to me in the morning.

The realisation has me scrambling to call Tash again. I know she wouldn't do that to me. But I need to hear it from her. She'd wanna answer her damn phone this time. I dial her number and listen to it ring and ring and ring…

'Hiya, babe! Sorry, I've been swamped. How are you?'

Oh, she answered finally. 'Hi, Tash.' Just those two words have her on edge.

'What happened? What's wrong?' She knows me too well.

'I saw the smile Mike had as you were leaving. He only smiles like that at me normally. I need to know what you said!'

Tash laughs – lord, I love that woman's laugh. 'Oh, Marie! I wish I could tell you, but I promised I wouldn't, and I am going to keep this secret for a little while longer. But trust me, please, it's nothing bad. You know I love you. I couldn't and wouldn't ever hurt you like that.'

Finally hearing her tell me that has all the stupid thoughts for the last two days disappearing and me laughing at myself for being a complete crazy lady.

'Please tell me you haven't been riding Mike too hard over that?' I can hear the admonishing tone she has.

'I, ahhh, well, I didn't mean to be… You know how I get… UGH! You should have just told me that two days ago!' I'm stumbling over my words, and she knows I've been on his ass for days over this.

'Oh, Marie, give that man a break! He loves you – let him have this secret!' She laughs at me, and we move on to what's been going on with her.

'Oh, honey, how are you coping with that?'

Tash is in tears and all I want to do is hug her. She had gone home to a massive fucking mess and isn't coping.

'I'll be okay. I will call you later, okay?' She's looking for an out and I am going to give it to her for now.

'Oh, babe, I am always here no matter what. I love you, Natasha.' I hang up the phone and cry a little.

Poor Tash has so much going on and yet still let me vent and get my head clear before she told me about her issues. She is an amazing person. She shouldn't have to do this shit alone but for right now she is okay. She would call me when she needed me; she always has and I've never turned her down yet.

I walk inside and see the time. Shit! Mike would be home in thirty minutes and I'd spent the day overthinking everything. I haul ass into the bathroom and have a quick shower. I do my hair and get dressed into something nice. As I walk out of the bedroom, I hear his truck pulling up.

'Hi, baby!' I say as he walks in the house.

He stops in the doorway and looks at me. 'Hello, beautiful! You look amazing!' He steps into the room, and I kiss him when he makes his way over to me. 'Let me get changed and we can go?' he asks as he walks towards the bedroom.

'Take your time, babe, I'm not going anywhere.' I smile at him, and he stops and looks at me.

'Something is different...' He watches me a minute and shakes his head.

'Nope, I'm the same as always. Happy my guy is here.'

I watch him walk to the bedroom. He looks back at me as he walks in the bedroom door.

'Are you sure everything's okay?' he asks before disappearing into the bedroom.

'Yes! Go get ready!' I laugh at him and when he is gone, I walk outside and roll a smoke.

About fifteen minutes later he walks out, and my jaw hits the ground. He has never looked like that before.

'Jesus, you're hot babe!'

He is dressed in black jeans, a black shirt and he has a black beanie pulled down over his hair. His thick silver chain is outside his shirt, shining at me and the green in his eyes is breathtaking.

'Ready?' he asks, and I nod my head as all other words have escaped me in that moment.

***

Mike

Walking into the room I pick up my phone and dial a number. 'Hi! Does she know?' Tash asks before I can even get a hello out.

'No, unless you told her!' I say, sounding somewhat unsure.

'I haven't said a word! I spoke to her earlier today and she was just caught up in her head. I fixed her.' Tash sounds happy with herself. But I can hear she isn't her normal self.

'Are you okay, Tash?'

'No, but you don't need to worry about me for tonight. Go.'

I say goodbye and hang up the phone.

I spend more time than normal getting ready. Marie looked stunning when I came home. I feel nervous and unsure as I continue with the finishing touches. I shake my head, no point worrying just yet, I don't know anything or how things will turn out. I'm not one for worrying about what will be or hasn't passed yet, that's all Marie's job. I smile to myself as I walk out of the bedroom and towards Marie.

***

Marie

I'm watching the scenery fly past the window when I realise we aren't going to where we would normally go. I look over at Mike and he is gripping the steering wheel harder than he normally would.

'You okay, babe? And where are we going?' I ask both questions in a blur of words.

'Yeah, baby, I'm good. And it's a surprise!' He grins at me.

His grin catches me off guard; it feels like forever since I've seen it. Although, I have been caught up in my head. I haven't really been myself since Tash left. However, after talking to her I know she's okay, dealing with a lot, but okay.

Mike pulls the truck over. We are literally in the middle of nowhere. I look at him and he grins a little wider. 'Come on, baby!' he says as he gets out of the truck.

I get out of the truck and he is standing there with a blindfold in his hand. 'Put this on and trust me.'

I trust him. I place the blindfold on as he takes my hand.

'I won't let you fall, just follow my voice.'

I follow his voice. We walk for a few minutes when he tells me to stand still and not move.

'Wait right here. No peeking! Promise?'

'I promise, babe.' I can hear the ocean but it doesn't sound close. It's kind of weird because no matter where you are on this island, the ocean is close.

'Okay, baby, take your blindfold off.'

I take the blindfold off and see we are at one of the lookouts. The moon is just rising and looks so big already. I look down and there's a picnic dinner by candlelight set up and there's Mike, kneeling. My heart jumps into my throat for a second.

'Baby girl, come sit with me.'

I walk forward as soon as I can make my feet move. I kneel down next to him and he kisses me.

'Happy anniversary, Marie!'

My eyes fly open wide. Has it been a year since I came here? When did that happen?

'It's been a year?' I must sound shocked because he laughs.

'Yes, baby!' He laughs again. 'I'm a little surprised you didn't know.' He nudges me.

'Happy anniversary, Mike!' I lean over and kiss him. I draw back. 'To be fair, seeing you kneeling threw me for a hot minute!' I look at him and I swear he blushes. Do I still make him shy?

He hands me a glass and we sit, eat, drink and talk for a few hours. We watch the moon rise, listening to the waves crash down on the beach and the lightning off in the distance. I lay back and look at the stars. There's so many, so different to the city. I haven't missed being in the city for a whole year!

'Marie?' His voice is quiet.

'Mhm?' I open my eyes and he is leaning in above me.

His hand cups the side of my face, turning my head slightly towards him. He leans in and his lips brush mine softly. His lips are just touching mine. Feeling when my hand finds its way into his hair, he leans in a little more, kissing me deeply, taking my breath away with it and making my insides turn to liquid. As the kiss continues, it becomes more passionate and, feeling his tongue in my mouth, searching and making me moan, I grip his hair more. I don't want it to end and try in vain to keep him right there on my lips. He pulls back just enough to look me in the eyes.

'Thank you for being a part of my every day, Marie.'

I smile at him as I pull his head back in to mine. 'I wouldn't want to be anywhere else, Mike.' I lick his bottom lip, enticing him to kiss me like that again.

As soon as his lips are on mine, I pull him onto me, my hands running down his back. I feel him press into me. Kissing me with more desire and want now, my lips are swollen. He continues kissing, slowly working his way to my neck leaving a trail of kisses along my jaw line. As soon as his lips lock onto my neck, I arch my back and push his head a little harder onto my neck. Feeling me melt into him, Mike starts undoing my shirt, running his hands down my side. He follows with his lips and tongue, slowly making his way down to my sweet spot. Every time I gasp or moan, he lingers in the spot that caused it. When his tongue finally touches my clit, I cry out softly, grinding onto his tongue, lips and face. I gasp as he enters me, as Mike moves with slow, soft movements. He makes love to me gently.

After, laying on the ground naked, we are breathless and happy. Mike looks over at me and I fight to meet his gaze through my hooded eyes, a lazy smile plastered on my face. There's no shifting it either.

'Marry me?'

That might have done it. I am holding my breath. I can't move or talk.

'Marie? I know you heard me.'

I finally remember how to breathe. I take a deep breath and turn my head toward him. I can only just make his face out in the moonlight and there's no way to see his eyes.

'Say it again.' It's all I can manage while I try to swallow my heart.

'You heard me just fine.' He places a box on my chest, drawing my attention. 'So answer the question.'

I can hear him suck in his breath; he is nervous.

'Okay.'

He is quiet for a long minute. 'What?'

'You heard me just fine.' I laugh at him.

He leans over me, placing his hand on the box I haven't touched since he placed it there and says, 'Say it again, Marie.'

I draw in a breath. 'Yes, Mike. I said yes.' I hardly have a chance to finish what I'm saying before he kisses me long and slow.

❧ *Chapter 22* ❧

A few days later, the ring box is still sitting on my beside. I haven't put it on yet and he never offered so it stayed where it was. In its box. I'm still in disbelief that he even asked, let alone bought a ring. It wasn't ever something we talked about. I mean, I haven't even told Tash yet. I should call her. I'm about to pick my phone up as Mike comes outside.

'There's my girl.'

I smile at him; he seems to be back to his old self.

'Hey. I think I'm going to call Tash sometime today. I haven't told her yet.'

'She knows.'

I look up at him sharply and he laughs at me.

'She was there when I got the ring.'

Of course she was! Everything clicks into place. The hug, his smile, the weirdness and Tash not being contactable – she is terrible at keeping secrets.

I smile a little wider.

'Why are you smiling, baby girl?'

I shake my head. It's getting late and decide to head in for a quick shower.

'I'll be back soon.' I kiss his cheek and walk inside. I hear him light his cigarette.

Warm water cascades over me in the shower, my thoughts drifting with the steady stream. My phone rings from the bedroom but I ignore it, enjoying my moment alone instead. Once I've finished, I pad barefoot into the bedroom to find Mike seated at the end of the bed. I walk over to him, my hair dripping on him. 'Baby, I'm getting wet!' he protests.

I smile. 'So am I, honey.'

Hearing that, he grabs my ass and pulls me onto him. I straddle him and, leaning down, I kiss him. I adjust my position slightly and feel him slide into me. I take my towel off, and he instantly has a mouthful of breast. I rock on him slowly, enjoying the feeling of him being deep inside me. I place my hands on his shoulders and grind down a little harder. Mike grabs my hips and pulls me down as I get closer. He wraps his arms around me as I cum.

'Ooooooh my god, baby.' I gasp as I drop my head down and kiss him long and slow, moving just enough to drive him crazy.

I feel his grip on me change slightly and he rolls me onto the bed.

'Baby, we are going to have wet sheets!' I complain.

Mike laughs. 'You should have thought about that before dripping on me!'

He crawls up my body, kissing me the whole way up as he makes it to my lips. I feel him enter me again and I thrust my hips up to meet his. I arch into him and move with him as he makes love to me. Long, slow, so much passion in the way he moves and touches me. Every little thing he does quickens my breathing, my moans get louder and my body responds only to his touch.

After, I am laying with my head on his shoulder. I kiss him. 'I'm going out for a quick smoke, babe. I'll be right back.'

'Okay, baby.'

I grab my phone as I leave the room. I smile over my shoulder at him. Heading outside, I look at my phone and see a missed call from Tash. I listen to the voicemail.

'Hey, Marie, call me as soon as you get this, please.'

I dial her number. 'Hi, Tash, what's wrong? You never leave voicemails.'

'Marie.' It's all she can get out before she sobs down the phone at me.

'Tash! Take a breath, babe. You've got time, honey. I'm not going anywhere.' Hearing her cry like that tears at my heart so much. Tash isn't a crier. I can't even fathom what would have happened to get her this point.

'Marie, I need you.' She sounds broken. My heart breaks.

'Tell me what you need and I'll be there, babe, you know that.'

'I need you here, with me – I can't, not alone. I'm sorry.' She hangs up.

She hung up! She didn't even tell me what was wrong. I finish my cigarette and try to call her back, but it rings out. She won't answer; she is closing herself off. So unlike Tash. She needs me there. I have no choice; she'd drop her whole life for me in a heartbeat and has done before. I need to go back to Australia. I need to be there for her.

I head back into the bedroom and Mike is asleep. I brush the hair off his face a little and kiss his cheek. I move around the room quietly. I don't want to wake him up. I see the ring box on the bedside table. I open it; this is the first time I've laid eyes on the ring. It's stunning. My heart lurches in my chest. I pick the ring up and put it on my finger for a second. I tear up. I place it back in the box.

I finish getting what I need and look at my guy again. I kiss his cheek and linger, taking in what he looks like when he is peaceful and sleeping. I can smell him; I savour it. I don't know when I will see him again. I'm all about family first and Tash has always been my only family.

I walk into the lounge and sit for a second. I check flights and there is one leaving tonight in two hours. I book the flight. It kills me a little that I need to go – it tears me up even more that I don't think I can wake Mike up to tell him. But for some reason I just know that Tash would freak if I showed up with Mike and I don't think he'd take no for an answer. I feel like I'm stuck between a rock and a hard place. I book a taxi. I cry, hoping with everything in me that he will listen and forgive me. I just know I have to be there for Natasha.

I write Mike a note and put it under the ring box. I hear the taxi pull up, I look at my guy one last time and turn and walk out, tears falling as I walk out the front door.

Mike,

I needed to go. It's Tash. I will call you.

I love you.

Marie xxx

The End

Shawline Publishing Group Pty Ltd
www.shawlinepublishing.com.au